Cold water coursed down Gage's neck and under his shirt.

"Me, too!" Cat took the hose and doused her face. No thought about makeup or hair. Just complete, natural joy. Scooping her wet hair from her face, she offered him the hose.

He took it, put his thumb over the end and sprayed a mist into her face. Instead of objecting, she turned around and lifted the hair off her neck, letting the spray wet her neck and back. "Ahh," she sighed.

He couldn't take his eyes off the intimate, natural pose she'd assumed. The pale nape of her neck drew his attention. Would she notice if he touched— *Stop!*

Pushing aside dangerous thoughts, he began watering. Cat inspected the shrubs they'd planted in the yard. His eyes discreetly followed her. What did Cat think of him? Did she only think of him as a business partner?

Books by Lyn Cote

Love Inspired

Never Alone #30
New Man in Town #66
Hope's Garden #111

LYN COTE

Born in Texas, raised in Illinois on the shore of Lake Michigan, Lyn now lives in Iowa with her real-life hero and their son and daughter—both teens. Lyn has spent her adult life as a teacher, then a full-time mom, now a writer.

When she married her hero over twenty years ago, she "married" the north woods of Wisconsin, too. Recently she and her husband bought a fixer-upper cabin on a lake there. Lyn spends most of each summer sitting by the lake, writing. As she writes, her Siamese cat, Shadow, likes to curl up on Lyn's lap to keep her company. By the way, Lyn's last name is pronounced "Coty."

Hope's Garden
Lyn Cote

Love Inspired®

Published by Steeple Hill Books™

STEEPLE HILL BOOKS

Steeple
Hill™

ISBN 0-373-87117-1

HOPE'S GARDEN

Copyright © 2000 by Lyn Cote

Printed in U.S.A.

"Consider the lilies of the field,...
even Solomon in all his glory was not arrayed
as one of these...if God clothes the grass of the
field which...tomorrow is cast in the oven,
shall He not clothe you?...But seek first
the kingdom of God and His righteousness;
and all these things will be added to you."
—*Matthew* 6:28-30, 33

With love and gratitude
to my dear mother, Catherine, and to Joy,
thanks for always living up to your name!

Chapter One

Two things had been on Cat Simmons's mind. Gage Farrell's handsome face. And a dirty undershirt.

The bright April sunshine made her squint. Pulling sunglasses from her breast pocket, she one-handed them on. Breathing in the sweet fragrance of freshly strewn cedar bark, she scanned the brand-new strip mall on the east side of Eden, Iowa. Her handiwork—the patchwork of well-placed blue spruces and evergreen shrubs in the reddish-brown cedar bark beds—needed only a border of red petunias to be complete. She would line the curb with the petunias after the danger of frost had passed in early May. Then everything would be symmetrical, colorful, harmonious.

She listened politely to the out-of-town contractor, just an average-looking guy, unlike Gage Farrell.

She knew the closing-the-deal routine from years of watching her late father sell nursery stock to retailers. Now this building contractor was trying one last time to get her to cut something off the price. Prepared for this, she'd built a five percent discount into her bid just as her father always had. She'd let the man talk awhile longer, then offer him two percent and hope he'd take it. Because she was a young woman, she knew she wouldn't be taken as seriously as her father would have been. This put her on her guard, so she kept her noncommittal "business" expression in place.

The contractor said, "I expected you to use more mature stock."

"You know my bid was the lowest because I grow most of my own stock. These shrubs have a whole growing season to establish themselves...." She went on speaking. Though keyed up, she didn't want to appear uptight. When the time was right, she'd bring the conversation to a neat end. She could do this.

Gage Farrell's face came up in her mind. Thoughts of him—hair the color of black walnuts, eyes the color of evergreen needles—had intruded on business all week. How was she going to hold her own against a college-educated business partner—a man who'd handled commercial real estate for nearly six years? He'd be more like the new yuppies moving into town, not like the longtime Eden people she felt comfortable with. A new partner now—right in the midst of all the changes in town... What had she been thinking when she signed the partnership papers? She blocked these thoughts.

The contractor said, pointing, "The shrubs you planted on the parking islands—"

She decided she needed to assert herself. "Are wintergreen barberry. Their spiny leaves and twigs will keep people from trampling them.''

Thinking of prickly things, a kind of internal twitch went through her. The closer Farrell's arrival loomed, the more often this irritating sensation zigzagged its way down her spine. A week from today, exactly, he'd arrive.

The contractor intruded, "Why did you choose blue spruce for the street-side island?"

Cat glanced at the contractor and sensed the time to end the "negotiation dance" had come. Though her stomach shook, she offered a two percent discount. He hesitated. She lifted her chin and offered three firmly. He nodded. They shook.

Climbing back into her white truck, which announced Hope's Garden in neat green lettering surrounded by vines, Cat breathed a sigh of relief. She'd done it, closed her first big commercial job!

The thoughts of her partner zoomed back into her mind. Even though they'd met only a few times at her cousin Laurette's house, he'd made an impression on her. Not the kind that would lead to wanting him as a partner. He wore all the right labels and had that big-city way about him as though life was his for the asking.

She usually stayed away when Laurette's husband, Chuck, had his college friends like Farrell visiting. She always felt out of place around guys who talked about college people she'd never met and laughed at jokes that made no sense to her. She hoped Farrell wouldn't act like that at the nursery.

She'd barely squeaked through high school, and her

father hadn't seen any need for her to even go to the community college in the next county. She hadn't wanted to go for more school anyway. Would not going to college work against her now?

This partnership was a risk she'd been willing to take. A bank loan would have needed collateral, her business. She hadn't wanted to do it that way, so she'd accepted Farrell's money and Farrell. She'd made her bed, now she'd have to lie in it.

With effort, she turned her mind to her list of things to do before her new partner arrived. She'd check all the greenhouses herself and she'd go over her ledgers one more time. She'd be ready for Mr. Big-City Partner.

After scooping her unruly hair into a ponytail, she drove down the road recalling the story of the dirty undershirt. Great-grandmother Catherine Hadley, whom Cat had been named for, had been twenty-nine and still unmarried. In spite of her father's protests, she had taken the train to western Kansas to be the mail-order bride of a farmer there.

Great-grandmother had stepped off the train. The Kansas farmer waiting for her had worn a clean shirt over a dirty undershirt. That had obviously said volumes to Great-grandmother. She'd gotten on the next train headed home for Iowa. The following year in spite of her banker father's disapproval, she'd married Cat's great-grandfather. His son, Cat's grandfather, had started the nursery Cat inherited from her father.

Next Monday Cat's own mail-order partner would arrive. Should she find a dirty undershirt and wear it to greet him? Cat grinned ruefully. She doubted Farrell would be that easily sent back to Chicago. No, her partner was coming to stay whether she liked it or not.

Back at Hope's Garden, she knelt in front of the sales area beside a halved, whiskey-barrel planter. With her hands deep in black dirt and the earthy scent of peat moss all around her, Cat grinned with soul-deep satisfaction. If the day continued bright and warm, the spring rush of customers would bury her in a happy, lucrative avalanche. She heard a car driving in.

She dismissed lingering thoughts of Farrell from her mind. Whimsically she sniffed the velvety green leaves of the geranium. She loved their pungent fragrance. *Creator of all, thank you for spring buds.*

"Hi, is the owner around?"

From under the bill of her cap, she glanced up to a man who stood over her, blocking the morning sun and casting her in his shadow. He was tall enough to make her look up, but then most everyone was. She stood up. Gage Farrell? *It couldn't be!*

The right side of Farrell's face was freshly scarred, a single red gash along his cheekbone. She'd heard about the accident. But the deep red welt startled her anyway. Not wishing to be rude, she directed her gaze to his green eyes. "Farrell?" she asked, her voice faltering. Without warning, naked pain arced in his eyes and touched something deep inside her, drawing her quick sympathy.

Farrell must have thought her uncertain welcome was in response to his scar. His greeting smile tightened. A non-committal mask slipped over his features. "Cat?"

She offered him her hand, realized she still had her gardening gloves on, and snatched one off. Studying him, she shook hands. Completely off balance, she said the only word in her head, "Hi."

She'd remembered Farrell as tall, dark and good-looking, but she'd forgotten the effect of the total package. Gage Farrell was drop-dead handsome. It would take more than a scar to change that. Wearing a slate-blue chamois shirt and tan twill slacks, he could have stepped right out of a luxury car ad. Except for his scarred cheek, she could imagine him smiling at the camera as he drove off in option-loaded comfort. Her stomach sank. *You're here a week early! My list!*

With arms folded and his eyes analyzing her in return, he said in a deep, attractive voice, "I got everything wrapped up sooner than I expected. So here I am."

She couldn't think of what to say. She couldn't say, "Come back in a week!" Why was he looking at her so oddly? Did she have dirt on her nose or something?

Behind him, three cars pulled in almost simultaneously. The dazzling spring morning was bringing out customers. She felt like wringing her hands. How could he do this to her?

"Cat!"

Both of them turned toward the sales entrance. Her purse on her shoulder, Cat's temporary help was speed-walking toward them. Dreading the answer already, Cat asked, "What is it?"

"The school nurse just called me. My twins have chicken pox!"

"Chicken pox?" Cat echoed. The sinking sensation in her stomach accelerated.

"Yes, I'm sorry, but I've got to go and take them home. I won't be back for a week or more!"

Cat could do nothing, but nod mournfully.

Two more cars pulled in and another five customers got out while her temporary assistant drove away.

"I guess it's good I came early," Farrell said, looking at the customers swarm around the bedding plants.

Cat nodded numbly. What next?

A customer waved at them. Cat's cordless phone rang. Farrell walked over to the customer.

Letting him go, she pulled the phone out of a pocket in the dark-green gardener's apron she wore over her jeans and plaid flannel shirt. Into the receiver, she recited, "Hope's Garden. We have every bloomin' thing you need. This is Cat Simmons. How may I help you?"

Laurette said in a weak voice, "Hello, Cat? Is everything going okay?"

"You didn't warn me Farrell was in town!" Cat accused her best friend.

"Gage arrived late last night out of the blue. You knew he'd be staying with me and Chuck."

"He's thrown me off completely. I wasn't ready!"

"I know. I talked him into calling you first, but you weren't in. He left here while I was being sick again. Cat, I'm really feeling awful today."

"Still nauseated?"

"Yes."

Sympathy filled Cat. Laurette, in the third month of her pregnancy, had been battling morning sickness, which kept her from working alongside Cat as she had for the past two years. Cat wanted to say, *Laurette, it's lonely without you here.* But she couldn't say that. Her cousin felt bad enough already.

"Be kind to Gage. He's had a tough year. Chuck's been concerned about him since we went to that funeral in Chicago after the accident. Come to supper tonight. It will help you two get acquainted away from work." Laurette moaned, "Oh…not again." The line clicked.

Cat sighed. What could she say? Nothing. She pushed a button and dropped the phone back into one of her many apron pockets. She glimpsed Farrell bringing a retired couple, the McCoys, into the windowed sales area, and she hurried to meet them at the counter.

Farrell walked in with a flat of bedding plants. Old Mr. McCoy said, "Now, young man, you're certain those are all sweet banana peppers? We got a hot one mixed in last year and planted it with the rest without realizing it. Ma canned the peppers in fall. When I opened a jar and bit in…whoo-ee!"

Farrell nodded with a slight grin. "Surprised you, I bet."

"You said it!"

I got my surprise today, too! Cat complained inwardly as she greeted the older couple.

"You want to ring up this order?" Farrell asked.

I suppose so since you don't know how! "Sure, but

I need to talk to you afterward.'' She shot him a look that meant she had something important to say.

"Likewise.''

Forcing a smile at the older couple at the counter, Cat accepted their payment. "You should have let us know about that mix-up, and we would have refunded your money.''

Mrs. McCoy shook her head no. "That's okay, Cat. Besides, the old man needs something to pep him up occasionally.''

This sally started a cheerful play argument between the couple who'd been married more than fifty years. It lightened Cat's mood momentarily.

Before she finished the sale, Farrell sauntered outside in answer to another customer's wave.

Bidding the McCoy's to come again soon, Cat rounded the corner of the desk to pursue him. She needed to show Farrell how things were done here. Her phone rang. Talking to a customer interested in adding hostas to her shaded yard kept Cat busy while she watched Farrell discuss a flowering crab apple tree with another female customer. She hoped he knew what he was talking about. Crab apple trees and commercial real estate didn't have much in common after all.

Hanging up at the end of the hosta explanation, Cat made her way toward them and smiled. "Are you able to answer all her questions? This *is* your first day on the job.''

"Oh, he's convinced me!" The lady laughed. "I'll be back when I'm ready to buy!" She waved goodbye to them, then drove away.

"Farrell, we need to talk about where things are. I wanted to give you a tour—" That's as far as she got. Another flock of customers landed.

Whenever Cat got close to Farrell, her heart sped up like a Geiger counter near radium. He made her more nervous than closing the deal at the strip mall. *This is not a good sign.*

In the midafternoon, they nearly collided, both of them with their arms loaded with flats of pink petunias. She said in passing, "I'm sorry we're understaffed today. I didn't intend to put you right to work. I knew I'd have to hire someone soon, but…"

"No problem. I'll handle it."

"Okay."

Later they passed again, "You know I expected to have another week to get ready for you." Her pulse beat faster from his nearness, leaving her more flustered.

"No problem. So far everything seems fine. When we have a chance though, I'd like that tour."

"Chuck said you did lawn work during the summers while you were in college?" she asked, casting for a more detailed explanation of his gardening knowledge.

"Don't worry. I know my way around growing things."

How did he have enough confidence to arrive at a new business and just move into action? His unexpected presence playing havoc with her concentration, she still wanted to ask for specifics, but didn't want to buttonhole him in front of customers who were gathering around them again. She lowered her voice, "Well, if you need help, don't hesitate to ask."

"Sure."

Customers claimed both of them once again. With a glance over her shoulder, Cat went off to explain the proper way to apply fertilizers. In spite of the obvious confidence Gage showed with customers, Cat still had her doubts. And she had no faith in a man asking for help. Her father would have died first. *Please, Lord, don't let him give the wrong advice to someone!*

After selling fifty pounds of rotted cow manure and loading the bags into the customer's truck, Cat passed her desk and prayed silently, *Lord, this isn't what I had planned. Calm me. Help me see clearly, be businesslike.*

She sighed and opened her eyes, then caught sight of the calendar and the date. April first. Her mouth turned up into a wry smile. "April Fool to you, Cat," she whispered.

At the end of the day, Cat rubbed her temples. She'd hoped for a busy day, and she'd been buried by the workload. Her two high school student helpers had arrived at 3:30 p.m. and had taken care of the plants in the greenhouses while she and Farrell had sold and sold. But just being busy hadn't given her a headache. He'd kept making her stammer and blush.

How would she get used to having Mr. Smooth working beside her? She'd never thought she was this susceptible, but Farrell had distracted her all day. She'd almost dropped a flat of marigolds on his toes and she put her phone down and forgot where. But he'd worked as hard as she and what she'd overheard him telling customers had been correct. And to be honest, she would have lost business without him. Customers weren't always willing to wait for help. But no one had gone away dissatisfied today.

Obviously, the growth in Eden had increased Cat's business faster than she expected. Seeing the business expand was great. But she had to make sure her increasing operating costs didn't get ahead of profits. And she might need another pair of hands to help out around the shop. Whom could she call to work her temporary assistant's hours until the chicken pox passed? And would Laurette improve enough to come back to work? If she didn't, Cat would have to rethink adding just one more full-time employee. She'd go over her budget and see if she could afford not one, but two new employees.

As always, she'd go slow and make sure she found the right person. She didn't want her new partner putting his two cents in on hiring. She'd lived in Eden all her life. Coming from Chicago, what would Farrell know about hiring someone in Eden?

She glanced at her watch—5:45 p.m. Only fifteen minutes until closing. The sun was sinking on the horizon. She'd never been so happy to see a day end.

Gage shifted on his feet trying to ease the weight off his sore leg. He'd always thought selling commercial real estate kept him busier than a human should be. But selling plants and answering questions made him as tired as if he'd been digging ditches all day. He'd tried to figure out where things were at the garden center without asking too many questions. He didn't want his brand-new partner thinking she needed to lead him around by the nose. He'd carry his own weight. Even on a bad leg.

A shiny, white sport utility vehicle drove up. A pretty blonde wearing designer jeans got out. "See, they're still open, Dex!"

Gage sized them up instantly. Definitely a *dink* couple—double income, no kids.

"I see. I see." The tall lanky man caught up with her.

The pretty blonde grinned. "When I saw the spring sun this morning, I just couldn't wait to get our garden started. I want it to look like one of those gardening shows on TV."

"Whatever, Samantha."

Drained after the nonstop day, Gage took a step and felt himself limp. He stopped. The lingering weakness was a constant reminder of the accident. Remorse gripped him, halted him. When he hung back, Cat stepped from the shadows and approached the blonde.

The contrast between the two women was sharp. The blonde was platinum, tall and slender, while his partner was compact, very shapely, with an abundance of sun-bleached hair pulled into a ponytail. Cat Simmons looked like the cuddle-up type, cute, but not his style.

Taking on a young female partner had worried him. Would she feel uncomfortable around his scar. So far, she didn't act like she did. But it had certainly put Daria off.

Cat said politely, but firmly, to the couple, "We're about ready to close. How may I help you?"

"We're the Crenshaws. Are you Hope?"

Cat smiled, but Gage thought it looked strained.

"No, Hope was my mother. I'm Cat Simmons."

"Cat, we just moved into our brand new house out in Paradise Hills." The blonde motioned eastward.

Cat nodded fractionally.

Gage shook his head. Didn't his partner know anything about the body language of selling? She had taken a combative stance and her tone sounded wary. Why?

He walked evenly toward them, feeling pain shoot up his leg. "Hello, folks." He shook hands with them both. "I'm Cat's partner, Gage Farrell. New house, huh?"

"A white Georgian with columns. I'm Samantha." The blonde grinned at him. "But everyone calls me Sam. This is my husband, Dex."

"She had to have columns," her husband added with a smile.

Cat spoke up, "What were you looking for?"

"We need to landscape," Dex replied.

Cat took a step closer. "Do you have a sunny yard or a shady one?"

Dex snorted. "Sunny. There isn't a stick growing on the property."

"A sunny yard is good," Cat admitted.

"Gage." Sam looked up into Gage's eyes. "Is it bad to have a shady yard?"

"I think she means that most flowers like sun. Isn't that what you meant, Cat?"

Cat nodded and shoved her hands in her back pockets.

Uncertain about Cat's reaction, Gage motioned for the couple to follow him. They stepped into the greenhouse. "I take it you're wanting to do something appropriate to a Georgian with columns?"

"Exactly!" Sam enthused.

Wishing Cat had a display of gardening magazines, Gage walked the couple through the closest greenhouse, discussing the merits of annuals and perennials in a garden. His partner trailed them, offering a comment now and then.

He noticed her rubbing her temples once. Maybe she had a headache. That would explain her uneasiness around these customers.

Finally, with a glance at his watch, he suggested, "Something like this takes thought. Why don't you buy some gardening magazines and bring them back Saturday morning around eleven? Then we'll get a better idea of what you're looking for."

"Sounds good." The husband drew his wife snugly under his arm. "Come on, Sam. We'll go to the new strip mall and buy some pretty flower magazines for you to drool over."

Cat bid them good-night and headed for the office.

So Gage shepherded them out to their car and waved them off. Then he went inside to face his partner. The aching in his leg taunted him and made him speak gruffly, "Did you take something for your headache?"

Cat walked to the door, locked it and switched off the outdoor lights. She faced him and said in a tired voice, "Oh, you noticed? I took extra-strength aspirin. That should take care of it. Would you like some?"

Until she asked this, he hadn't been conscious that he was rubbing his sore leg. Hoping she wouldn't ask him any questions about it, he stopped, then glanced at her. "Maybe later."

"Okay. I'm nearly done here."

No more questions? A woman who didn't pry? Leaning against the counter, he realized, in spite of his pain, he felt better than he had for a long time. Just working with plants again had made him forget some of what had happened in the past ten months, made him feel alive again. He fingered the small cross that hung around his neck, the one Manny, his old boss, had left him.

"You must think I'm completely disorganized," Cat stated.

Her frankness impressed Gage. *Well, please don't hold back, partner.* "Not at all. So far everything looks in good shape. Chicken pox isn't your fault." But he understood the thought behind her point. "I didn't mean to put you at a disadvantage by arriving early. If you hadn't needed me today, I might have gone home. But I'm glad I was able to help. What did we take in?"

Cat knew he had a perfect right to ask her this question, but it still irked her. With effort, she kept her voice neutral. "Uh…$879.62." She walked to her desk and began putting the neatly separated and rubber-banded sheaves of cash into the zippered bank bag.

"Not bad for April first. Is this normal business for a spring day?"

"No, we're busier than usual. Part of it is the unusually warm weather and part of it is the new population."

"If this pace keeps up, we're really going to need help. Hopefully we'll have someone soon. I called in the help-wanted ad."

Cat froze. "You what?"

"I called the local paper and put in an ad. You know the usual, 'Help wanted. Hope's Garden.'"

"You didn't!"

He looked at her as though she'd sprouted a second head. "You said you were sorry to be understaffed. I said I'd handle it. You said okay. So I just went ahead and took care of it."

Her temper flared. She wanted to hit him. Over the head. With something heavy.

He leaned on the counter across from her. "Just hiring one more person may not be enough, though. We may need another part-time person, too."

Still holding back her sparking temper, she resented his using *we*. There had been no *we* about calling in an ad. She said slowly and firmly, "When you said 'I'll handle it,' I thought you meant the work. I didn't want to put an ad in the paper yet."

"Why?" He looked surprised.

"This isn't Chicago." She chose her words carefully. "Eden is a small town, and this is a small business. I don't want to have to turn down someone I know, but who wouldn't work out here. I normally use word of mouth to find someone. You should have asked me before you called the paper.''

"I see," he conceded. "I'm used to running a large agency, calling in an ad was routine."

She nodded grimly. "In the future, I think *we* should discuss decisions like this."

He eyed her as if he were waiting for the next shoe to drop, then nodded. "Okay. Sorry. Thought I was helping."

"Okay." Frowning deeply but without another word, she zipped the bank bag shut. "I called someone to come in tomorrow to help out till the pox is over."

Nodding, he stood up straight. "Need me to do anything more before I leave?" he asked in a conciliatory tone.

Cat glanced at him. He looked beat, and she'd noticed he'd tried to hide that his leg was giving him trouble. "No, that's all right. I'll just go around and check to see if everything is locked up and shut down."

"I can do that."

"No—"

"I said, I'll do it."

She wanted to point out he looked like he needed to sit down, but she didn't think he'd appreciate it. Men didn't like women to point up their weaknesses. She'd learned that from her father. Dad had ignored symptoms until he died of an early heart attack. "There's a checklist of closing duties on the inside of the back door. If you need to ask a question, call me or Laurette. She knows the routine.''

Farrell nodded.

''I'm going by the bank's night deposit drop. I'll see you at Chuck's. Laurette invited me for supper, too. Just push the button lock on the door when you leave.''

''Will do. See you there, partner.''

Cat clenched her jaw and walked out into the spring evening. She'd known she wouldn't like having a partner. Especially one used to running things his way.

Cat pulled into Chuck and Laurette's driveway beside their traditional white Cape Cod. She'd driven straight over from the bank. She parked and walked through the garage and into the kitchen. ''Hi, it's me!''

Immediately the house felt odd. Too quiet. No aroma of a dinner cooking. Cat hurried through the kitchen, dining room, then called up the stairs, ''Laurette!''

''Up here!'' Chuck yelled.

Cat raced up the stairs. She found him sitting on the floor of the bathroom clutching Laurette in his arms. ''What's wrong?'' She fell to her knees on the cold vinyl tile and reached for her friend's wrist to find a pulse.

''I just got home and found her here on the floor.'' Chuck eyes looked wide and wild.

''Is she breathing?'' Cat nearly choked on the words.

"Yes."

"Did you call her doctor?"

Laurette's eyes fluttered open. "Cat?"

"What's wrong?" Cat squeezed her hand.

"I feel so weak," Laurette said in a breathy voice. "I tried to get supper started…I couldn't. I can't even keep water down."

Cat stood up. "I'm calling Dr. Nelson."

"Good. Hurry." Chuck hugged Laurette closer.

The fear that this might be more than just faintness, that it might be the first stages of miscarriage made Cat rush into the bedroom. As she dialed, she prayed a frantic litany, "God, take care of Laurette and her baby. God, take care of—"

A woman's voice answered her.

Cat plunged in, "Laurette Halley, a patient of Dr. Nelson's, passed out at home and just regained consciousness. She says she can't even keep water down."

"Any bleeding? Is she having contractions?"

Cat called these questions to Laurette. "She says no. She's just light-headed and nauseated."

"Is there anyone else with you?"

"Her husband."

"As long as she's conscious, have him put her in the car. Dr. Nelson is already at the hospital checking on another patient. I'll call and tell him you're on your way." *Click.*

Cat hurried to Chuck to help him get Laurette to her feet and down the stairs. While her own heart fluttered like a captured bird, she held Laurette's arm tightly and repeated her prayer over and over.

After helping Chuck lay Laurette in their car, Cat stood, bereft, in front of the garage and watched him drive away. "I'll tell Farrell, then I'll come right away!" she shouted after him. She shivered and wrapped her arms around herself. Nothing bad would happen to Laurette, she told herself firmly.

Before Chuck's car was out of sight, Farrell drove up the street and pulled in beside her. "What's up? Where's Chuck going?"

Cat stepped close to his car. Her voice trembled. "Chuck found Laurette unconscious. He's driving her to the hospital."

"Which way?"

She looked into his green eyes and saw her own concern reflected there. For a second, she felt connected to this man who'd raised havoc with her peace all day. "Follow me."

"No, get in. I'll drive you."

Cat didn't argue. Her head had begun throbbing, and she didn't trust herself to drive. For the first time all day, she was glad to let Farrell take charge.

Chapter Two

Sickened by the odor of disinfectant and by her throbbing head, Cat paced the brightly lit waiting area outside the emergency room at the community hospital. Chuck and Laurette were in one of the white-curtained areas where Dr. Nelson was examining Laurette.

Farrell sat hunched on a faded tan plastic chair a few steps away. With his elbows propped on his knees, he rested his head on his fists. For the first time, Cat noticed he wore a chain around his neck with an intricate gold cross. She wanted to look at it closer but held back. They were almost strangers, and Farrell didn't appear to invite attention.

For the moment, all of Cat's irritation over Farrell's high-handedness had been shelved. As she paced the worn, but polished gray linoleum, tears gathered in her throat. Laurette and Cat's mothers had been first cousins. Laurette and Cat, born two months apart, had been inseparable ever since. *Dear God, please don't let anything happen to Laurette and her baby. Please.*

As she paced by Farrell again, he murmured, "Can you hear anything?"

Frowning, she paused and shook her head, careful not to jar her aching head.

Surprising her, he leaned forward, took her hand, and tugged her to the chair beside him. "You're worrying too much."

His presence bolstered her. She'd paced this same linoleum after her father collapsed with his fatal heart attack only two years before. That night he'd been in the greenhouse working late as usual. Thoughts of that dreadful evening haunted Cat now. "But anything could go wrong...."

"Chuck told me they have a great doctor."

She stared at him. Farrell looked deeply concerned, but that shouldn't surprise her. Though he'd rarely visited Eden in the past five years, he'd been Chuck's friend since their freshman year together at college. "I know, but—"

He went on, calmly holding her hand, "And Laurette hasn't had any trouble other than this persistent nausea, has she?"

"No, but something must be wrong." She knew she should pull her hand away, but his soothing touch kept her sitting still beside him and took the frantic edge off her concern. A desire to rest her head on his shoulder flashed through her mind. She closed her eyes, stiffening her independence.

"It's probably just dehydration," Farrell offered. "She hasn't been able to keep enough food down. If you went a few days without eating, you'd faint, too.''

She probed his steady gaze to judge the truth of his statement. Did he mean it or was he a person who just said polite things? "You think that's all it is?"

He nodded. "Any food scent at all seems to set her stomach off. This morning Chuck brewed our coffee in the garage and that's where we had to butter our toast." He gave her a half smile.

Grateful he wasn't making light of her concern, Cat smiled at him. "Laurette will make a great mother."

"They'll both make great parents." Farrell's voice, firm and rich, soothed Cat more. Suddenly she realized Farrell still held her hand. His long, slender fingers cradled her hand with unexpected tenderness. Being so close to Farrell whispered through Cat's senses. How strange that he could comfort her now when all day long she'd wanted to send him back to Chicago.

Down the hall, Dr. Nelson and Chuck stepped outside the curtained examining area.

Farrell stood up, pulling Cat to her feet. She didn't draw away. His nearness strengthened her. Chuck nodded and shook hands with the doctor. Cat's knotted nerves tightened. She couldn't hold back any longer. "Chuck?"

His thick brown hair disheveled, Chuck hurried toward them. "No need to worry! Laurette and the baby are fine."

"Then why did she pass out?" Farrell asked.

"Her nausea caused her to become dehydrated."

Cat looked up at Farrell beside her.

He met her gaze with a teasing glint in his eyes.

Though her fears had diminished, only willpower held her from running to her cousin. "Is she conscious?"

Chuck took a deep breath. "Yes."

"Can I see her?" Cat took a step forward.

Chuck touched her arm. "They're keeping her overnight to get her body fluids and electrolytes...whatever back on track. I have to do paperwork for her admission. Cat, why don't you go—"

"I'll go to her." Cat hurried down the hall, then slipped through the opening between two white curtains.

Laurette held out her hand.

Cat grasped it in both of hers, then leaned down to kiss Laurette's sunken cheek. Her cousin's loveliness had taken a beating. Her long, blond hair was flattened like a cornfield after a hail storm, and her large blue eyes had gray smudges underneath. Cat said what she thought, "You're a mess."

Laurette chuckled weakly. "Please don't mince words. Tell me exactly what you see."

"Don't tease. You scared me—us—to death." Still holding her cousin's hand, Cat stroked a few errant strands of hair away from Laurette's pale face. Touching her reassured Cat that everything was all right.

Laurette smiled. "I'm sorry. I still can't believe being pregnant has hit me like this. Don't worry. Everything's going to be fine."

Cat nodded. "But you've been so miserable. I just wish I could do something for you."

Laurette squeezed her hand. "Help keep Chuck's

spirits up. I think he's more worried than he should be.''

"What did Dr. Nelson say?"

"I'm just one of those unfortunate women who, though perfectly healthy, doesn't have an easy time being pregnant."

"I thought he said you'd be over your morning sickness by now."

Laurette blinked her eyes as though warding off tears. "Most women are, but evidently not me. I don't remember ever feeling this weak. *Don't* repeat that to Chuck."

Handing her friend a tissue, Cat struggled not to worry Laurette by looking too concerned herself.

Laurette wiped her tear-moistened eyes. "How did Gage's first day with you go? I worried about you being upset. I know how you hate surprises."

"We didn't argue." Cat mentally crossed her fingers in the hope this would continue. "For a first day together, it went fine. Farrell worked hard."

"Glad to hear you say that, partner." Farrell, a step behind Chuck, entered the curtained area. His grin teased Cat as though daring her to say more.

"Well, good." Chuck eyed them both.

Cat hoped Farrell didn't think she'd been talking behind his back and was relieved when two attendants entered to wheel Laurette toward the elevator.

Cat and Farrell trailed behind the procession. When Cat glanced up at Farrell, she found him studying her.

In an undertone, he said, "This has been a hectic day, but we'll work things out. I have a lot of ideas for Hope's Garden, but we don't have to talk business now.''

Cat's rising mood lowered. He had ideas for the nursery? What ideas? But her hands recalled his gentle touch. She should have pulled away. She had never let someone, almost a stranger, touch her like that. Did he think she was a helpless female because she'd shown emotion?

The next morning in the nursery sales area, Cat stood glaring at Farrell. Another sunny morning mocked her. Inside her, storm clouds gathered. ''You *what?*''

''I preinterviewed a person while you were gone,'' Farrell repeated. He faced her, his back propped against the open front door of the nursery, his black-brown hair tousled by the spring wind and his pine-green eyes watching her react.

Did he think this was a game? ''I thought I explained yesterday how hiring should be handled.'' Crossing her arms, Cat tried to keep her response low-key, but firm.

''I didn't hire or fire anyone. She showed up, asked for an application. When she was done, I read it and asked her a few preliminary questions.''

Every word he spoke so calmly made perfect sense, but she didn't like any of them. Having this man sticking his fingers into her business...correction, their business... She took a deep breath and tried to ignore the ungainly rhythm of her heart. ''What's her name?''

''Thetis Quinn.''

"What?" Frustrated, she raked her fingers through her ponytail. Didn't he remember anything she'd said yesterday about the ad?

"You heard me."

To Cat, the name spelled *faculty wife* in black capital letters. How could she say to her fresh-from-the-big-city partner, but I'm a "townie?" He couldn't be aware of the timeless tensions between the townspeople of Eden and the faculty and students of the one-hundred-year-old, small liberal arts college. She never felt at ease around the college people.

From behind, Cat heard a breathy feminine voice ask, "Did I hear my name?"

Cat turned to view Thetis Quinn. Her premonition appeared to be accurate.

Slightly older than Cat, Thetis wore small round spectacles like Ben Franklin, no makeup, a denim jumper over a madras shirt. Untamed, curly hair the color of red wheat touched her shoulders. Beaded earrings, transparent balls of amber and red, dangled from her ears.

The woman held out her hand. "I'm Thetis. And I would love to work here."

Cat shook her hand, then took a step back toward the desk behind the counter. "I haven't had time to read your application." She didn't want to be unfair to the woman. Maybe she would pan out.

Cat observed that Farrell hung back. Was he going to let her do the interview? Had the preinterview been enough for him?

Thetis smiled, showing winning dimples. "I just wanted to introduce myself. I know today is busy for you, but my husband's buried alive correcting term papers. When I saw your ad this morning, it was kismet.''

"Oh,'' Cat said cautiously. She could feel Farrell's concentration on her, not Thetis. She hated the warm blush he aroused in her. She unnecessarily straightened a few papers on the counter beside her.

Thetis continued enthusiastically, ''Yes, I've been so restless lately. Unable to concentrate on preparing my lecture notes. Everything has been dry as dust to me—*even* eighteenth-century English love poetry! Can you believe that? Then I saw your ad. Hope's Garden—what a glorious name!''

"Oh?'' Cat asked, not feeling good about this. Eighteenth-century love poetry? How did that prepare someone for gardening?

Farrell stood just behind the woman, trying to hide a grin. *Very funny, Farrell.*

"Because here I am blooming with life.'' Thetis patted the front of her jumper. ''Just two months. I'm not showing yet. But I feel so…Earth Mother. And suddenly I knew I needed to be around growing things. Fecund earth called to me!''

"Really?'' Cat said, not knowing what *fecund* meant, but suspicious of it. It sounded like a dirty word. She hated not knowing more from books, but she'd never been good at school. She bet Farrell knew what *fecund* mean. He stopped hiding his grin. He *was* enjoying this. The warmth of Cat's flushed face increased.

"So I came right over to apply. I really want this job.'' Thetis motioned grandly toward the nearest greenhouse. "It will be perfect, and the growing season will be over before I deliver. I'm only teaching part-time till May first, then I'm off for a year. But working here is just what I need to be doing while I'm carrying my first child."

"But do you have any gardening experience?" Cat asked, trying to keep up with the woman's enthusiasm.

"Yes! My own dear mother always says she 'raised' me in a garden!"

"Really?" Cat walked to her desk and leaned one hand down on it. In this conversation, she needed something solid as an anchor.

Farrell advanced, still lingering behind Thetis, still smiling. Cat wished she could wipe that smile off his face. Where was a lemon cream pie for throwing when one was really needed?

"She is a horticulturist, and my father is a botanist! I've worked with plants all my life!" Thetis pointed to one of the barrel planters beside the open door and began reciting the Latin names of the flowering pink-purple-and-silver plants in it, *"Ageratum houstonianum, Dianthus, Lobularia maritima, Sempervivum tectorum."*

"Well...good," Cat stammered, knowing she'd lost control of the interview. She pictured the yellow cream pie splatting on Farrell's face, dripping down his square chin. She swallowed with difficulty.

"The name of your nursery...Hope's Garden, such symbolism for an expectant mother!" Thetis gazed at Cat hopefully.

"Uh-huh," Cat muttered. Outside, two more cars

pulled in. A friend from church was filling in for the temporary assistant who was home with sick twins. Another frantic day. She needed to get this "interview" over.

"I couldn't resist coming right out." Thetis leaned forward.

"We're glad you did." Farrell ambled forward and leaned against the counter.

Ignoring him, Cat interjected, "Don't you think this might be too much for you as your pregnancy progresses? There's a lot of lifting, bending and stooping...."

"I haven't had a bit of trouble! Not a sick moment!" Thetis opened her arms wide as though hugging the world.

Cat took a step back. "But wouldn't you rather spend time in your garden at home?"

Farrell folded his arms, still giving Cat that teasing look.

"We live in an apartment. I have only a window box! Real estate prices have jumped so high in the last two years since the Venture Corporation moved here. The money I'd earn here this summer will augment the remainder of a down payment for our first house!"

Farrell straightened up. "I don't think we can say no then, can we, Cat?" His voice held a hint of amusement.

"It's just minimum wage. Are you sure?" Cat objected futilely. How had she let Farrell get her into this fix? She needed time to think this over!

Ignoring her hesitance, Farrell shook the lady's hand. "You're hired, Thetis."

Cat gritted her teeth against putting into words what she was thinking about Farrell.

Thetis squeezed Farrell's hand, then jigged over and squeezed Cat's. "Thank you, but please call me Hetty. All my friends do. I'm teaching only two night classes this semester. When should I start?"

Fuming inside, Cat said firmly, "Tomorrow." She hoped twenty-four hours would be enough time for her to cool off and be able to welcome Hetty properly.

Hetty thanked them both again and popped out to her little red foreign car and drove off.

Hands on her hips, Cat stared at Farrell pursing her lips to hold back hot words. But the angry red scar on his cheek tugged at her, softening her exasperation.

Farrell said mildly, "That takes care of hiring a full-time employee. The ad did the trick."

"How could you hire a space angel like that?" Cat asked. She had to admit she'd been impressed by Hetty's enthusiasm, but her partner had just been lucky.

"She's eager, pleasant, knowledgeable—"

"Just being able to recite the Latin names of the stock," Cat growled, "doesn't mean a person knows anything about working at a nursery."

"Hey, she was 'raised' in a garden by a horticulturist and a botanist." His smile broadened.

Was Farrell going to be just as controlling as her father had been? Men liked to run things, be in charge. It was a fact of nature. Capitulating, Cat slumped down into her chair behind the desk.

Farrell spoke briskly, "We need to get outside now. So for the record, I won't call in an ad or even preinterview anyone else without you. But we needed to hire more help and it's still early in the season. And Laurette doesn't look like she'll be back anytime soon, so we may need someone else. I know you said Eden's a small town, but it's time you stopped thinking small-town. With Venture Corporation here and two more software corporations near to relocating in Eden, you need to start thinking bigger."

Cat stared up at him. What did he know about Eden or her family's hard-won business reputation? Her father had killed himself to build up this nursery. But she said coolly, "My main concern is to keep my—*our* bottom line in mind. Expanding too quickly could put the business in jeopardy. And for your information, Hope's Garden has been and *still is* the best nursery in this county."

"Fine. But your clientele is changing and so must Hope's Garden."

Listening to the buzz of evening visitors in the hospital hallway and nearby rooms, Cat fidgeted on the chair beside Laurette's bed. Laurette had begun having contractions and had been kept at the hospital for observation. Now, Wednesday evening, after two days of hospital food, Laurette had requested a hot fudge sundae, so Chuck and Farrell had left to buy her one. Cat was relieved Farrell was out of her face. At work, away from work, she couldn't get away from him. In her mind, she kept seeing him tell Hetty she was hired. And it irked her more every time.

Laurette stared at Cat. "You don't look happy. Is it me or Gage?"

Still worried about Laurette but unwilling to show it, Cat made a face. "Farrell."

"Gage is a nice guy. Just give him a chance."

"I am." *Do I have a choice?* Cat switched topics. "Are you sure you're ready to go home?"

"I'll be fine. I just have to stay off my feet, so I don't start having contractions again." Laurette continued, beginning to sound glum, "Tomorrow I'll be home and on the couch for the rest of the month."

"You sound as cheerful as I feel." Cat had mentally crossed Laurette off for the rest of the summer as far as working at the nursery. She'd ask the two people who were filling in if they could stay for the season. In the morning, Cat would face day four of the partnership. What would Farrell spring on her tomorrow? "You don't like staying home anymore than I like adjusting to a partner."

Laurette grimaced broadly.

A large, raw-boned woman wearing blue jeans and an intricately quilted vest over a denim shirt, hustled into the room. "Now don't do that. Your face might freeze that way!" The woman chuckled.

"Aunt Bet!" Laurette and Cat exclaimed in unison. Aunt Bet, a lifelong neighbor of Laurette's, was the closest thing they had to a grandmother.

Aunt Bet, sixtyish, robust, gray-blond, hugged first Laurette, then Cat. "Where are your menfolk? I want to get a close look at that new fellow, the handsome devil who's turning heads in town."

Handsome devil! If you only knew! Cat gave up her

seat to Bet, moving onto the wide windowsill next to it.

"They went to get ice cream," Laurette replied. "Thanks for coming."

Aunt Bet took Cat's chair. "I've stayed away. I knew the whole neighborhood would be in to see how you are!" She delved into her hand-quilted denim purse, pulled out a pack of gum and offered each of them a green-wrapped stick.

Bet chewed gum incessantly and always offered it to others. The scent of spearmint made Cat's mouth water, but she shook her head.

Bet put the extra stick away. "Laurette, your mother called from Florida. We talked it over. Chuck can drop you off in the mornings. You're spending days at my place until you're on your feet again."

"Oh, that's so sweet," Laurette exclaimed, her blue eyes lighting up. "But I can't tie you down like that."

"Not to worry." Aunt Bet held up her hand. "If I have to go out, May Perkins or Doris Lutter will pop over. All your neighbors want to help out. We have nothing better to do."

"I don't believe that!" Laurette objected. "You're busy all the time quilting and working at the library with kids."

Aunt Bet glanced sideways. "Cat, you look like you're sucking a lemon. What *is* the matter?"

"She's adjusting to having a partner," Laurette tattled sweetly.

"But such a partner!" Aunt Bet teased, patting her breast pocket as if to say, "Be still my heart."

"I wish Gage could hear you say that. Sometimes I think he's self-conscious about the scar." Laurette sighed.

Did good looks mean so much? Even to Aunt Bet who'd stayed single her whole life? Cat muttered, "Go ahead. Make fun of me. You've never let a man tell you what to do!"

"That's why I never married or got myself into a partnership with a man. What's he done to get your garters twisted so soon?"

Cat smiled grudgingly. "He put a help-wanted ad in the paper without asking me." Her complaint sounded trivial to her own ears.

"I wondered about that ad," Aunt Bet mused.

Encouraged, Cat jumped up. "That's just it! I always ask around before putting an ad in the paper. And you won't believe who he hired full-time."

"Who?"

"A college professor, Thetis Quinn." Cat put her hands on her hips.

"I know her." Aunt Bet smiled.

"You do?" Cat asked in surprise.

"She joined my quilting circle this winter. She's very talented and a lot of fun. But about this new partner, you never were one to like change, any change," Aunt Bet said sagely. "Give the guy a chance." Aunt Bet turned to Laurette. "And *you're* getting started on that baby quilt tomorrow bright and early!"

"Oh, thank you! I forgot you promised to help me!" Laurette beamed.

A particle of envy stuck in Cat's throat. Laurette

was married to a wonderful guy. Now Aunt Bet would help her make a quilt for her first baby. Did Laurette know how lucky she was?

Laurette spoke up, "Stop frowning, Cat. You're overreacting. You needed to hire more help. Gage found someone."

Was Laurette right? Was she making a big deal out of something small?

Aunt Bet pointed a finger at Cat. "You know, your dad, God rest his soul, was the most bullheaded man I ever met."

"You got that right." Shoving her hands in her jeans pockets, Cat swallowed her chagrin with effort.

"So this Gage Farrell should be easy for you after working with your dad."

"You got that right." Cat repeated, grinning wryly in spite of herself.

Aunt Bet chuckled. "Remember, '*Men*—you can't live with them. You can't live without them.'"

At that moment, Chuck and Farrell walked in with two white bags. They proceeded to lift out five, plastic-domed sundaes. The rich fragrance of fudge filled the room deliciously.

"I told you someone would show up while we were gone." With a warm smile, Chuck handed Bet the fifth sundae and a red plastic spoon.

"See! Men even come in handy sometimes." Bet nodded her thanks and took a big bite of whipped cream and nuts.

Flushing red-hot, Cat couldn't look at Farrell. He must know she'd been talking about him. It had been stupid of her. She knew better, but he did twist her garters every time they were together. But was he to blame for this or was she?

On Saturday morning returning from a stock delivery, Cat opened the door of her truck and came face-to-face with her partner. "Farrell," she gasped, startled at their sudden closeness.

Farrell nodded toward the sales area. "Looks like the Crenshaws are keeping their eleven o'clock appointment. Let's go."

Reluctantly Cat walked with Farrell away from her truck but paused at the flats of tomato varieties near the front door. With her head bowed, she listened for Farrell to work his "magic." If the past week meant anything, he'd have Samantha Crenshaw eating marigolds out of his hand within minutes. Cat knew she should be grateful that her partner knew how to handle customers like the Crenshaws, but his easy masculine charm intimidated her.

Farrell shook hands with the couple. "Hi, Samantha, Dex. What did you bring me?"

The pretty blonde waved an armful of glossy magazines. "Gage, I had so much fun with these! I never knew there were so many flowers to choose from. I never even saw some of these in California!"

Cat shook her head. *Big surprise.*

Farrell chuckled. "The Midwest has a bountiful variety of flowering plants. Now, what did you like in particular?"

He could sound so appealing, but did he mean it? How did he turn his charisma off and on so easily? Cat asked herself.

Sam opened a magazine and showed him page after page of flowers—ageratum, coreopsis, hydrangea, on and on.

Does she want a garden the size of a national park? Cat smirked down at the yellow tomato blossoms.

Finally Farrell held up his hands in surrender. "Okay, we need to set up an appointment to go over your property." He turned slightly. "Cat, let's get them on the calendar."

Ill at ease, Cat walked over. Hope's Garden had moved into commercial landscaping with Farrell's money, but residential jobs were still new to her. "Mr. and Mrs. Crenshaw, why don't you come inside and look at some photo layouts of the gardens I've supplied locally? Then we'll schedule an appointment."

Sam looked to Farrell. Farrell nodded and motioned her to follow Cat.

Sam's dependence on Farrell irked Cat even though she understood it. Inside, she pulled from a drawer some scrapbooks that served as her garden portfolios. Even her father had admitted she had the touch for garden design. She motioned Sam to sit down opposite her at the desk. "Take some time and look through these while I look over the work schedule."

As Cat pulled out the large calendar, she felt as though she were creeping on unstable ground. Most of her customers traditionally had worked on parts of their property trying different plants and combinations of annuals and perennials over many years. But those customers had bought previously owned properties.

The new population in the three brand-new subdivisions had different needs. Their lots were empty, blank slates that needed complete landscaping. She could adjust herself to meet this challenge, but she wouldn't let Farrell suggest some standard cookie-cutter garden to customers.

Farrell spoke up, "Cat and I will come out to your place, test the soil, look at your drainage, your structure and the different aspects of your whole property, then we'll draw up a couple of different proposals."

Cat resented Farrell taking charge, rolling over her like a lawn tractor, but she couldn't let this show.

"That sounds like just what we need," Dex said.

With a shy glance at Cat, Sam put in, "I plan to take care of the garden myself after it's in. I want some outdoor activity while Dex is off golfing."

Dex snorted. "Yeah, since it's almost a forty-five-minute drive to the nearest course. You'll have *plenty* of time for gardening!"

"A forty-five-minute drive?" Farrell looked surprised.

"That's right," Dex repeated.

"Gardening is wonderful exercise. What's a good date, Cat?" Farrell walked the couple toward the door.

His smooth voice grating on Cat's sensitive nerves, she suggested, "How about Friday after five?"

Because of business travel, the Crenshaws moved the appointment to a week from Sunday, waved happily and left. Farrell joined her beside the counter. Cat opened her mouth.

Farrell interrupted her, "Cat, you have to get rid

of this idea of mainly working with farmer's wives and weekend hobbyists.''

"That's not the point here. I won't have you doing one-size-fits-all gardens for yuppies. Hope's Garden has a reputation to live—''

"Your negative attitude toward the Crenshaws comes through loud and clear.''

This stopped her. "It does?''

He leaned within inches of her. She caught the clean scent of his soap. "Chuck explained to me the changes here, the new people moving in. I know the Crenshaws aren't what you're used to, but they're customers and their money will be accepted by the bank.''

Cat pursed her lips, irritated with herself that she'd allowed her feelings toward these people to intrude on business. She was letting her own bias against the changes in Eden, her hometown, affect her business judgment. She nodded, avoiding his gaze. "You're right.''

He leaned closer still. His appealing smile began melting her defenses. "Cat, you knew this nursery had to change or be left in the dust. Did you hear a nursery in Mount Pleasant is planning to start a store-front on Highway 218 to sell their stock to this area? You needed my money to expand into larger land-scaping jobs, didn't you?''

Pulling away from him, she tried to shake the downturn in her spirits. "I needed your money to ex-pand, but facing change isn't easy for me." Making changes and having to consult with Farrell daily kept her fuse short.

He nodded, then turned to walk away.

"Wait." She gripped his arm, stopping him. Awareness of him coursed up through her fingers to her arm. Embarrassed by her reaction to him, she stammered, "Hang this up." Sweeping his jacket off the counter, she did a double take. Pointing an accusing finger at her desk, she demanded, "What's that?"

Chapter Three

"Sorry." Apologetically Farrell took his navy windbreaker from her.

"What is that *thing* doing on *my* counter?" Cat felt herself break into a cold sweat.

"It's just my laptop computer, and it's on *your* counter because you're the only one here who has a desk." His tone was easygoing though he raised an eyebrow at her.

A computer! Cat frowned at him darkly. Why did he keep popping things on her? And why a computer of all rotten things?

Looking unfazed, he considered her in return.

His intense gaze made her flush. Nervously, she tugged at the elastic band in her hair, tightening her ponytail. "So why did you bring your computer here?"

"Because you didn't appear to have one." He gave her a coaxing smile.

"We don't need a computer. This business has existed since 1930 without—"

"Cat." Farrell heaved a deep sigh, letting her hear his frustration. He dropped the jacket on the counter and put his hands on his lean hips. His gaze held a challenge and his masculine confidence taunted her. "Do we really need this discussion? A computer will help us keep a constant inventory, simplify bookkeeping and give us all kinds of advertising possibilities. You use a Bobcat not a shovel, don't you? A modern business needs modern equipment."

She chewed her bottom lip and fought back tears. Tears! She never cried over things at work.

Grabbing up the computer, he stepped around her and sat down at the desk. The chair creaked. He flipped open the black, rectangular laptop, tapped a button and the screen flared to life.

Folding her arms stubbornly, she kept her face expressionless. Inwardly, she felt like garden soil being stirred up by a rototiller. *Of course,* Gage Farrell had used computers routinely in his Chicago office. What would he say when he found out she'd never even touched one?

"This software is the latest in 3-D landscaping." He tapped a few more keys. Music played. A screen showing a lush green and flowering garden and blue sky came up and announced, "Garden Designer Deluxe."

It grabbed Cat's interest.

"With this program, you can plan a whole garden, then print it out for the customer."

So that's what this was all about! Her jaw hardened. "You mean like the Crenshaw's property?"

"Yes," he said evenly. "We can use it for hobbyists who want an overall plan to follow. Or we can use it to draw up custom plans for residential or commercial sites."

Cat wouldn't meet his eyes. She couldn't admit she was completely ignorant about computers. It hurt too deeply. He'd think she had just crawled out of the Stone Age.

Outside, two cars drove up, giving her an excuse to avoid the issue. "We'll talk about it later."

She turned. Out of the corner of her eye, the allure of the gardening screen on the computer caught her notice one last time. But she couldn't face telling Farrell the truth. She wasn't smart enough to master a computer.

"Don't say it." A few days later Cat held up her hand like a cop stopping traffic.

Farrell went on anyway, "I've kept my peace about the Hope's Garden tradition of preschool tours, but—"

Cat waved her hand in front of him. "Stop!"

They had worked side by side for over a week now, a bumpy week. Today had been a hectic morning. She didn't blame Farrell for being exasperated. Two rambunctious four-year-old boys, little Johnny Hansen and Sammy McCoy, had slipped away from their teachers. In the midst of their unsupervised exploration of one of the greenhouses, a fight had broken out. The crash of plants, boards and clay pots had brought everyone, even customers, running. After profuse apologies, the teachers had gathered up their charges and left early.

She put her hands on her hips. "Haven't you figured out why we do these tours every year?"

"It's good community relations, but we could do this in winter when—"

"It's more than that. These tours may be inconvenient sometimes, but they are definitely good business." *I'm so tired of having to explain things. Defend my way, Lord.*

"Prove it." Farrell raised his chin at her.

She led him to her desk. She opened the drawer and lifted out a sheaf of receipts with little yellow coupons attached. "Recognize these?"

His glance said, *Why are you asking me dumb questions?* "Yes, those are the little vouchers," he spoke with exaggerated patience, "which say 'Six bedding plants for one dollar' that each child gets at the end of the tour."

She answered in kind. "Right. Did you realize that the average amount that one of these brings back with it is $12.42?" She waved the receipts at him.

"What?" He stood straighter.

"At least, that's the figure from last year. I won't be able to average this year's coupons and receipts until the tours are done." With one hand on her hip, she indulged herself with a hint of a smirk in her expression.

"So *that's* why you give these out?" He stared at her.

"It was my mother's idea." The smirk left her

face. "She wanted every little child in Eden to be able to have even a little garden. She said any parent can afford a dollar."

"And usually more than ten dollars," Farrell conceded.

Cat shoved the receipts back into the drawer. Farrell's black laptop sat on the counter, mocking her like a large garden beetle she couldn't quite squash. Farrell hadn't said anything more about it, but it came to work with him every day. And sat staring at her. Was he trying to wear her down? Well, it was working. *I go home twice as tired as I should be every night, Lord. At this rate, I won't make it till fall!*

Looking outside, she saw a station wagon drive up. Four gray-haired ladies in flowery print blouses and dark slacks stepped out and pointed at the blue hydrangeas. Just in the nick of time! "Farrell, you'd better go outside. You do so well with senior citizens. Especially the ladies," she added wryly. "I'll clean up." She needed to be free from his disturbing presence.

"Are you sure?"

Cat nodded and pushed him to go. *Not a good idea.* Touching Farrell affected her like too much sun, leaving her flushed and a little shaky. She brushed this thought away. She'd be immune to her partner before she knew it. *Yeah, right.*

"Okay. One of us needs to be out front." He paused and gave her an apologetic look. "Sorry I sounded so angry."

"That's okay." As she walked away, she felt as though the taunting computer were making faces at her behind her back. How long was she going to be able to avoid that issue?

"Hi, Cat." Hetty approached with a sympathetic expression.

Cat smiled glumly. "Need something?"

"I came back to help you clean up." Hetty tucked a strand of reddish hair behind one ear.

Cat looked at the devastation around her, cracked rust-colored clay pots, potting soil and wilting, orphaned seedlings. "That's all right. I'll do it."

"No, I insist." Hetty knelt and began tenderly picking up plants that needed to be repotted.

Glad of the quiet and the absence of Farrell, Cat swept the dirt and broken pieces of clay pots into a pile, then picked up the boards and laid them back on the sawhorses, which made up the extra makeshift tables needed in the spring.

A glance at Hetty told Cat, once and for all, this new employee was qualified to work at a greenhouse. She was correctly sorting and gently repotting the young plants. Cat smiled with approval.

Hetty grinned in reply. "I overheard what your mother said about every child having a garden. That was a beautiful sentiment."

Cat kept her head down as she worked. But she agreed wholeheartedly. Her father had been a difficult man to work for, but whatever her mother, Hope, had said had been gospel to him. Cat had never doubted his love for her mother. She treasured that fact. "I was just quoting my father." Her voice became husky. "My mother died when I was only four years old. I have very few firsthand memories of her."

"I'm sorry to hear that."

Cat was extremely relieved that the woman asked no more questions. This Memorial Day, for the second year, Cat would be arranging flowers on two graves, not just one. She'd lost both parents before she turned twenty-one. Deep inside, a silent sob shook her.

Cat began sweeping more vigorously, letting the work eat up her grief. Soon everything was back to normal. "Thanks, Hetty."

"You're welcome." Hetty made no move to leave. "Bet Fisher said she is a relative of yours."

Cat glanced at Hetty and smiled. "That's right. You know Aunt Bet."

"I just love her! When I first moved to Eden, I tried to get acquainted with some longtime residents. But I didn't have much success."

Cat looked down feeling a touch of shame. She hadn't been very welcoming to Hetty herself.

"Anyway, after I got to know Bet at the town library, she invited me and another professor to join her quilting circle. I'm learning so much. Bet is so funny."

Cat didn't doubt that. Aunt Bet's sunny spirit left no room for gloominess. "I'm glad." And Cat meant it.

At church on Sunday morning, Cat sat in her usual pew, but alone. Laurette still couldn't walk and Chuck had stayed home to keep her company. Cat smoothed her blue cotton dress. Her father had always made some disparaging comment when she wore a dress.

She was only now realizing that he hadn't known how to cope with raising a daughter alone. When she had looked more feminine, it must have made him uncomfortable and that was why he'd discouraged her. But on Sundays and special occasions she wore dresses, even though she still had difficulty feeling at ease in a skirt.

During the announcements, the ushers seated latecomers. Startled, Cat observed Farrell in a dark, expensive-looking suit walk past her. With Aunt Bet at his side, he took a seat a few rows ahead. Farrell at church? The idea hadn't crossed Cat's mind.

Guilt jabbed her like a sharp thorn. Just because she'd had difficulty getting used to working with him didn't mean she didn't want to see him at church.

However, having him in plain sight just a few yards away, would make it harder for her to concentrate on the service. Was it just his good looks or his self-confidence that threw her? Without any effort, Farrell still seemed to "twist her garters" as Aunt Bet would say. *Garters? I'm in church thinking about garters of all things. If anyone read my mind, they'd think I was nuts. Gage Farrell is driving me nuts, Lord.*

The deacon at the front reading announcements caught her attention. "The new summer small-group youth program will begin as soon as school is out. We'd like to thank these couples who volunteered to shepherd four young people for the summer." He read off the names, which included Laurette and Chuck.

Cat frowned. Would Laurette be up to handling four teens when school let out in a month? Cat sent another prayer for God's blessing on Laurette's pregnancy.

The pastor approached the pulpit, prayed, then opened the large red leatherbound Bible. He read the parable of the Good Samaritan. This story was one Cat had listened to and read countless times. The traveler, beaten and robbed by thieves, was passed by, first by a priest, then a Levite, both of whom should have stopped to help him. But a lowly and despised Samaritan had stopped out of pity and had cared for the injured man. Who then had been the traveler's neighbor? The one who showed kindness. The central question, ''Who is my neighbor?'' echoed in her mind.

Hetty's words came back to her. *When I first moved to Eden, I tried to get to know some longtime residents....* The words had embarrassed Cat at the time. Now they burned in her conscience. Just because Hetty had been associated with the college, Cat had written her off. But honesty compelled Cat to admit that hiring Hetty had been a good decision.

Forgive me, Lord, for prejudging Hetty.

What about Farrell? her conscience prompted.

Acknowledging another direct hit, Cat fidgeted in her seat. Every Sunday, she felt as though she brought a charge card with accumulated debts to church. Here, she opened her heart and asked God to cancel each outstanding charge on her spiritual account. Then she could face each Monday, fresh and clean, prepared to meet the week's challenges.

Now, looking at the back of Farrell's dark head, she owned up. Her charge account was fuller than usual. She'd been irritated with him for two weeks. Jealous of her domain—which Farrell legally owned forty-nine percent of. Had she expected to take on a partner and have nothing change at all? She grimly confessed her error again, but this time promised to improve. *Sorry, Lord, I've been the pain in Farrell's neck.* She'd have to change her attitude and her ways big-time this week.

Her conscience pressed on, what about the Crenshaws?

Ouch. Cat squirmed uncomfortably on the pew. She'd been judgmental, territorial and short-tempered for two weeks. Closing her eyes, she prayed silently for forgiveness.

When she opened her eyes, she was able to concentrate on the rest of the sermon. At the end, she stood with the rest of the congregation to sing the closing hymn, "Trust and Obey." The line, "Never fear. Only trust and obey," heartened Cat. She promised silently, *I'll do better this week, Lord. With your help.*

Outside church as usual, people lingered greeting each other, exchanging hugs and watching the children play tag. Cat embraced Aunt Bet. Then while Aunt Bet chatted with two other women from her quilting group, Cat turned to Farrell who stood beside her. She was very aware that many eyes were glued on Gage Farrell.

Usually that phrase tickled her funny bone as she imagined cartoon eyes popping out and sticking to someone. But did all the attention make Farrell feel out of place? He stood a little apart. Did he think the glances directed at him were impolite? The truth was, scar or no scar, he was too new and too striking to be overlooked. Conscious that people were watching, she tried to appear as though they were talking business. *Well, it's the truth!* "You're going to the Crenshaws this afternoon?"

Looking surprised, he nodded.

"Then you'd better pick me up," she said bravely. "I live right on the way to Paradise Hills."

"Sure," he replied. But he stared at her as though trying to read her mind.

Cat took a deep breath and plunged on, "I was wrong. You're right. I've given you a hard time about the Crenshaws, and I shouldn't have. It's just business. I shouldn't let my personal bias enter into it."

Gage stared at her. "Well...great." Dressed in a simple, blue cotton dress and with her abundant sun-bleached hair worn loose, Cat affected him differently than she did at work where she wore jeans, a green garden smock, a matching billed cap and a ponytail. The Sunday-go-to-meeting Cat was more of a kitten.

By the end of their first week, he had decided his partner was going to remain a thorn in his side. That's what made her turnabout now catch him unprepared. What had changed her mind? He didn't have a clue. But he couldn't doubt her motives. Cat Simmons couldn't hide her feelings or opinions. This pleased him while making him uneasy at the same time. A woman like this would expect...demand complete frankness in return. He had concealed his hidden sor-row and uncertainty for so long. Would he be up to this challenge?

He nodded. "Okay. I'll pick you up around one-thirty."

"Good."

"Good." He wondered if this new attitude would extend to his laptop. And she'd been touchy with the Crenshaws before. Just how frank would she be with them today? He'd have to be on his toes every minute.

Chapter Four

Puffy white picture-book clouds drifted overhead against the delft blue sky. The warm breeze from the open window blew into Gage's face. When he saw the roadside mailbox, he turned off the county road to Cat's place. The black mailbox looked ancient and battered with Simmons nearly worn off. It didn't look like a mailbox Cat would own. Ahead, miniature spring-green leaves fluttered over mature maples and oaks. With trunks at least three feet in diameter, these aged giants hovered around the plain white, two-story farmhouse. Again, the house didn't jibe with Gage's preconception of where Cat would live.

The weathered wood siding was chipped and flaking, the front porch listed to the right while its steps listed to the left. Unkempt lilac bushes, shoulder-high, festooned around the foundation and clematis vines engulfed the screen porch railings up to the sagging, sad-looking gutters. In contrast, every aspect of

Hope's Garden was clean, neat and well-kept, just like Cat herself. What explained her living in this broken-down old farmhouse?

Then he noticed that the steps were painted a glossy dark green. Along one side of the steps, large clay pots of bright-pink geraniums adorned each ascending step. The screened-in porch had brand-new screening and held an arrangement of freshly painted white vintage wicker. Bright floral cushions on the furniture caught his eye. Now those touches looked like Cat's work.

As he drove up to the half-circle drive in front, Cat stepped from inside onto the porch, then down the wooden steps. He was surprised to see Cat still wore the blue cotton dress she'd worn to church. A flowing skirt gave her a new disconcerting appeal. He got out and opened the passenger side door for her. "Cat."

"Farrell." She gave him a restrained smile and slipped by him onto the front seat.

The wind lifted a few strands of her long hair lightly against his face. He detected the fragrance of some mixture of herbs and blossoms. Cat in a skirt smelling sweetly also didn't fit the conclusion he'd already decided about his partner. He'd put her down as one of those no-nonsense, independent women who dispensed with frills and femininity. Obviously, Cat Simmons was more than met the eye.

He got in and drove back down the gravel lane to the county road. "These trees look really old."

"My great-grandfather planted them."

"So this is where your family has lived for four generations?"

"Yes." She shifted in her seat. "Unfortunately or fortunately—" she waved her hand back toward the house "—my father was much more interested in the business than in modernizing our family's home."

He heard the embarrassment in her tone and it touched him. "Maintaining an older home can be quite expensive and time-consuming."

"Yes, and I hate that it's really been left too long. Sometime in the future, I plan to build a new house. I'd like a ranch along the river."

"A ranch?" he teased. "Do you mean a one-story house or a house with stable, horses and cowboys?"

She flushed pink.

Why was she blushing? Had he touched a nerve without intending to? He glanced at Cat from the corner of his eye. Her thick, sun-streaked hair fell into natural waves to her shoulders. Golden freckles dusted her upturned nose. No lipstick enhanced her naturally pink lips. The urge to touch her soft, downy cheek with the back of his hand nearly caused him to reach out. He reigned in his reactions. *Business.* Keep your mind on business, he told himself.

"Paradise Hills is just around this bend." She pointed ahead to the right.

He nodded as he drove into the entrance of the upscale subdivision. Uneasiness trickled through him. This morning after church, Cat had thrown him a curve ball, then a good Sunday dinner at Aunt Bet's with Laurette and Chuck and a lovely spring day had lulled him into a false sense of security. Now he'd been picking up confusing clues from Cat. This appointment was business, but he didn't know what to expect. Cat's last meeting with the Crenshaws hadn't gone easily. Would today go any better?

He shook his head. Evidently even life in Eden presented challenges. Glancing at the address on the card beside him on the seat, he drove to Sam and Dex's white Georgian with columns. He parked in front of their three-car garage. Cat got out without assistance and met him at the back of the vehicle. Suddenly the disparity between Cat's home and this brand-new megahouse registered in Gage's mind. Was this one reason for longtime residents like Cat to feel ill at ease with the newcomers?

Wearing a white Greenpeace T-shirt and cutoffs, Samantha stood in the open doorway. "You're right on time!"

Cat waved, but said nothing as she walked forward, obviously scanning the acre lot around the house.

Samantha called over her shoulder, "Come on, Dex! They're here!"

Smiling, Gage hurried up the few steps. He shook the hand Dex offered him, greeting them both warmly.

All the while, Cat mounted the steps looking around, expending no effort to make contact with the Crenshaws.

"Hey, partner," Gage bantered to cover her aloofness. "What do you usually do first on a home visit?"

She turned to him and nodded at the couple. "Let's walk the land." She dropped her leather purse to the steps, bent and took out a small brown cloth pouch and clipboard. She motioned for them to follow her.

Gage waved Samantha and Dex ahead. They caught up with Cat easily.

Cat began, "You need to buy a lawn fertilizer and herbicide system and apply it."

"Fertilizer?" Dex objected, "I thought the soil here would be especially rich."

"It is, but they stripped off your topsoil—"

"They what!" Sam sounded shocked.

Cat shrugged. "Sometimes when a farm is sold for residential use, the developer strips the topsoil and sells it. Topsoil is too costly to waste on grass."

This blunt statement of fact wouldn't put the Crenshaws in a positive mood and a positive customer was much more likely to spend money. Gage tried to think how to stem this topic, but short of clamping his hand over Cat's mouth, he couldn't.

Dex scowled. "That really burns me."

Cat motioned toward the hilly pastureland where Black Angus and white-faced Herefords grazed just behind Paradise Hills. "Look at it this way. Farmers were angry when this land was subdivided. To them, houses on prime acres is just a waste."

"We didn't think about that," Samantha said in a subdued voice. "We would never do anything ecologically harmful."

Gage groaned inside. *Oh, great. How to make the customer feel lousy.* "People have a right to a place to live." He made his tone humorous and tried to catch his partner's eye. "Your family, Cat, has lived here for four generations."

"Oh!" Cat looked startled. "I didn't mean to make it sound like you weren't welcome here."

"Four generations!" Sam squealed. "You're a real Iowan, then."

"Yes," Gage continued smoothly, "you've heard of the Hadley House—"

"You mean the one here in town that was just added to the National Register of Historic Homes?" Sam asked.

"That's the one. Cat's cousin was telling me that their great-grandmother was a Hadley."

Cat grinned ruefully. "Yes, Catherine Hadley disgraced the family by marrying my great-grandfather Joshua Simmons in 1900. The Hadleys were bankers and thought themselves better."

Sam looked impressed. "Wow! How cool. Dex and I didn't know what Iowa would be like. We almost didn't take the jobs here. But we love living in this beautiful unpolluted environment. No smog. No traffic. I can hardly wait to sample the fresh vegetables— especially some great Iowa potatoes!"

Cat's mouth dropped open.

Gage spoke up to prevent Cat from saying something less than polite, "Iowa farmers grow some potatoes, but Iowa is really known for its corn, hogs and beef."

Nodding, Cat closed her mouth.

"Really?" Sam looked unconvinced.

"Sam," Dex added, "Idaho grows potatoes."

"Oh, that's right!" Sam laughed at herself. "I always get Iowa, Idaho, and Ohio mixed up!"

Gage knew both Sam and Dex were software engineers. He began to wonder if Samantha was one of those people who were good at their jobs, but remained forever fuzzy on other topics.

As though changing subjects, Cat strode onward with firm steps. "Now the first thing we need is to take some soil samples. I'm pretty sure what your soil needs, but it's always good to make sure." She knelt down, opened the brown pouch and took out a tiny spade.

Gage stood beside Cat ready to give assistance if needed. His leg pained him, but he stood evenly, ready to stoop if necessary.

"Can I ask you a question?" Sam watched Cat intently.

Cat nodded as she dug up soil and put it in a small vial, sealed it, then marked it.

"When we flew here in the early winter, some farmers were still taking in corn from their fields. Why didn't they pick it when it was fresh? I mean, who wants dried-up old corn?"

Cat's head snapped up.

From where Gage was standing, he caught a flicker of a smile on Cat's face. Turning more toward Cat, he winked at her.

She answered him with a look, then she bent again over her work. Her voice came out muffled. "You're thinking there's only one type of corn, just the sweet corn that humans eat. Dried field corn is eaten by hogs and beef cattle. You've heard of corn-fed Iowa beef, haven't you?"

"You mean the animals eat it dried?" Sam didn't sound convinced.

Gage nodded but didn't let his amusement at Sam's

misconceptions show. Again a new thought came to him. Could this ignorance of Cat's hometown and state possibly be another reason why Cat had been so hesitant to work with newcomers?

They followed Cat to three more locations where she dug up small soil samples.

"What are you testing the soil for?" Samantha asked as they found themselves back near the front.

At last, an intelligent question! Gage was relieved.

"Soil can be alkaline or acidic. Too much either way can hinder plant growth." Closing the pouch, Cat rose. "Now we need to step inside."

"Inside?" Samantha sounded surprised. "Do you do houseplants, too?"

Gage held his breath and gazed into Cat's eyes.

At first, Cat looked puzzled, then her face cleared. She gave him a quick nod. "Yes, we do sell houseplants in winter. But now I need to see the different views from your windows, so we can plant what you'll enjoy seeing outside every day."

"What a great idea!" Sam clapped her hands.

Cat motioned Sam to take the lead.

Gage began to relax. So far his partner had impressed him by doing a very professional job in spite of the customer's naive questions.

Sam led them inside the oak-trimmed foyer. "What would you like to see first?"

"Where do you spend the most time in the house?" Cat peered around to the rooms that opened onto the high-ceiling entry.

"You mean when we're not sound asleep?" Dex

asked dryly, leaning against the bottom of the oak balustrade.

Gage knew that feeling. He and Cat usually put in twelve-hour days. But he'd done sixteen-hour days in Chicago sometimes.

Cat nodded.

"We often sit by the sliding doors at the back of the great room." Samantha motioned for them to follow her as she led them to the rear of the spacious, white-carpeted first floor. "We like to watch the sun set over the rolling hills. You know we thought the Midwest would just be plain flat. Why do we have hills here?"

"The really flat land is farther west," Gage offered.

Cat took up the topic. "We're in the Mississippi River Valley. Over time, all the rivers flowing to the Mississippi carved out valleys, forming hills."

"How interesting!" Sam exclaimed.

The house, done in neutral shades of beige and white, was sparsely furnished, but this didn't surprise Gage. "How long have you two lived here?"

"Six months. We just haven't had time to shop for anything." Samantha indicated antique chairs around a trestle oak table. "I want to decorate with antiques, but that takes time."

"Not if your family's lived in one place for four generations! My house is furnished in antiques." Cat smiled wryly. "You should drive north near Interstate 80. The Amana Colonies have tons of antique stores, and the Amish in Kalona make and sell traditional furniture. My Aunt Bet goes up there often."

"Do you think your aunt Bet could recommend some shops in the Amanas?"

Cat nodded and offered Aunt Bet's phone number. "Now how much did you want to spend on landscaping?"

Cringing at Cat's bluntness, Gage spoke up, "Can you two give us your ballpark figure?"

The couple exchanged glances. Dex mentioned a number. "We were hoping you would come up with a basic design that we could add to or subtract from."

"Since your time is limited, I would suggest that I design a patio garden outside the sliding doors because this is where you'll get the most pleasure from it." Cat's commonsense approach reassured Gage again. His partner lacked polish, but she did know her job.

"What about the front? I wanted something really eye-catching there!" Samantha urged.

"I'll plant some colorful shrubs like dwarf burning bush and a showcase circle of annuals in the front for your neighbors to enjoy," Cat granted. "Especially marigold and zinnias. They're great for cutting and bloom all season."

"What about trees?" Gage asked, watching to see how Cat would react to his taking part. Once again he found himself comparing the two blond women. He found his gaze lingering on his partner.

"Oh, yes," Samantha agreed.

"You'll need some to the west of your patio." Cat indicated a point to the right of the windows. "Something that will grow quickly."

"Why there?" Dex asked.

"Windbreak from westerly winds, especially in winter," Cat answered promptly. "And shade from the hot sun on summer afternoons and evenings. One last question."

Gage frowned, hoping Cat wouldn't undo all the good she'd done with this one last question.

Cat gazed around. "Your home is very formally designed, but you don't seem like formal people. Do you want a formal garden or a more relaxed design?"

Dex and Samantha exchanged glances.

"Can we have both?" Samantha asked tentatively. "Formal in the front and more casual around the patio?"

Cat nodded. "Certainly."

"Can I ask you another question I've been wondering about since I moved to Iowa?" Samantha asked diffidently.

Gage could hardly wait to hear this one.

Her eyes cocked toward Gage, Cat tilted her head. "Yes?"

"What are pork bellies?"

Cat looked startled. "You mean like on the commodity reports on the radio?"

Samantha bobbed her head.

"Pork bellies can become bacon." Cat's voice showed her uncertainty over this unusual question. She looked to Gage.

He shrugged.

The young woman looked a bit sick. "Pork bellies are bacon? Yuck. I wish I hadn't asked." She held up her hand. "Don't tell me what part becomes sausage."

Grinning, Gage offered his hand to Dex. He'd spare Sam the description of stuffing ground pork and spices into hog intestines. Evidently Sam knew little about food before it reached her table.

An unpleasant thought struck him. Did Cat classify him with the Crenshaws as just another yuppie? Did she think he was just as ignorant about Eden? This sobered him, but he brought the appointment to a businesslike end. "We have new garden software. I'll send you a printout of our proposal within the week." He noticed that Cat's face fell.

In spite of Sam's questions, the meeting had gone well. What could possibly be bothering Cat now?

Later that Sunday afternoon Cat walked warily into Chuck and Laurette's cheery, yellow-and-white kitchen. Her realization this morning in church that she'd been at fault in her attitudes toward Hetty, the Crenshaws and especially Farrell still had her unsettled. The appointment with the Crenshaws had gone better than she'd thought. Sam's questions would have irritated her if God hadn't prepared her earlier by reminding her that the new people in town, no matter how different, were still her neighbors.

But one more challenge hung over her. After Farrell's parting mention about a printout, she realized she couldn't put it off any longer. He'd made up his mind that she was going to use the computer. She'd have to tell him the truth that she wasn't smart enough to use a computer. The very thought of revealing this made her queasy, just like she had always felt before tests at school.

She pushed the disquieting sensation away. Right now she needed to get Laurette's house cleaned up. Laurette had always been neat as a pin, and Cat wanted to ease her cousin's fretting over what wasn't getting done. But she knew Laurette would insist she not do the cleaning, so she'd plotted with Chuck to drive Laurette to the riverside park for the afternoon. Alone, the house felt empty. Farrell must have gone with them to the park.

The mess in the kitchen didn't look as bad as Cat had anticipated. Someone, Chuck or Farrell, had been washing dishes and sweeping, but the stove and counters needed tidying. Enjoying the peace of the empty house, Cat began scrubbing the counter, then tackled the top of the stove. The fragrance of the lemon-scented cleaning gel filled the small kitchen. Then she heard the front door open and the sound of familiar uneven footsteps—Farrell.

For the third time that day, Cat braced herself to face him. Her anxiety over the computer threat struggled with the attraction to him she'd begun to dread. Today at the Crenshaws, she'd been so aware of him. She hoped the Crenshaws hadn't noticed that. She'd worked hard to appear professional. Conflicting emotions churned through her like a river high with melted snow and spring rain.

"Hi, I didn't expect to see you here." Farrell stood in front of her.

Farrell—handsome, insistent, but elusive. In the two weeks they'd worked together, he'd asked her no questions. He'd offered no personal information. That's the way she wanted their relationship, wasn't it? The specter of his black laptop computer wafted through her mind.

Cat swallowed to moisten her dry mouth. "Chuck took Laurette for a ride. I'm trying to get things spruced up before she gets back and tries to stop me."

"But I told Chuck I insisted on hiring someone to clean until Laurette is feeling better. It's the least I can do since they're letting me stay here."

Though she wasn't looking at him, his presence worked on her like an invisible sci-fi "tractor beam" trying to catch her attention. It troubled her. "Hiring someone's easier said than done."

"What do you mean?"

"There aren't too many people who clean houses for pay in town, and the few there were have been snatched up by the new executive wives. How's Laurette today?" She paused and looked at him. Day by day, she'd prayed every time Laurette and her baby came to mind. And they'd come to mind often.

"She seemed the same."

Cat nodded, then wiped every surface she'd cleaned with a fresh cloth.

Farrell stepped closer to her.

His formidable presence intimidated her. She looked away, suddenly bashful at having this man, still a puzzle to her, so close.

He put his hands on his hips. "All right. What can I do?"

"You don't—"

"I'll help you. I'm staying here. I would have moved out, but Chuck insisted I stay—"

"It's good you've stayed to support them." Cat glanced tentatively at him.

He stared at her.

She returned his look without hesitation, drawing strength as she always did from speaking the truth. "Having you around has helped Chuck. I'm glad you're here in the house to encourage him. Evidently God knew Chuck would need a friend right now." Flustered by his nearness, she walked away to wipe the crumbs off the dinette table.

Farrell cleared his throat. "I said I'd help. What do you want me to do?"

For the first time, his persistence pleased her and pushed back the worry over the computer. Taunting him with a playful grin, she propped one hand on her hip. "Know how to vacuum?"

He grinned back at her. "Yes, I'm afraid so," he drawled. "So, where's the vacuum?"

"Coat closet opposite the front door."

He lifted one eyebrow. "How do you know this house so well?"

"This is where Laurette grew up. I was here after school practically every day."

"All right." He saluted. "I'm off to vacuum."

As she finished the kitchen, she heard the welcome sound of the vacuum, first in the living room, then up the hall to the stairs. Glad to be free of his unnerving presence, she took out Laurette's bright-yellow feather duster and worked her way through the small living room and up the stairs.

Awareness of Farrell skittered through her as she stepped around him while he maneuvered the noisy vacuum into the master bedroom. Being alone in the house with Farrell affected her differently than working with him at the nursery. They were alone, no Hetty, no customers swarming in and out.

Here there was too little space for such a forceful man. He made her feel…softly feminine. Why was that? She shook her head and went on with her work.

The vacuum fell silent, and she heard movement coming out of the bedrooms. She turned. "If you're done in there, I'll just dust the bedrooms—"

"I'll dust," he offered.

The intimacy of sharing such homey tasks touched her. She turned sassy to cover her confused reaction. "Know how?" She offered him the feather duster.

He took it, then twirled it between his fingers. "Child's play." He "feathered" her nose with it.

The playful touch sensitized her to him even more. When she looked into his eyes, she glimpsed more than playfulness. Farrell was studying her to discover…what?

Cat's mouth went dry. She couldn't speak.

Still grinning, he "dusted" the underside of her chin.

She looked away as a small sneeze escaped her.

"Bless you."

"Thank you." What was going on between Farrell and her? At work, he saved his charm for the customers. At work, he treated her with a studied coolness she couldn't fight or penetrate. She turned to the staircase. "I'm going to the kitchen to weed out any moldy leftovers from the fridge."

He soon rejoined her downstairs and stood nearby

washing his hands at the sink. She paused, watching the soap lather over his long, sun-browned fingers. More than a week of gardening had taken its toll on his hands. With broken nails and dirt embedded around his cuticles, his hands now looked more like working man's hands, like her dad's hands. She sank into a chair in the dinette and wondered if his hands were calloused like hers. For no apparent reason, she imagined how they would feel against the nape of her neck. She shivered.

He turned off the tap and dried his hands, all the while looking at her. Why did he seem to study her so? Finally, he broke the silence. "So now, Cat, is the house clean enough?"

Unable to speak, she nodded.

He sat down across from her.

Again, she noticed the gold chain around his neck. He wore it every day. Obviously it was a memento, not jewelry. Daringly she reached out and lifted the cross with her index finger. "This is special to you," she said. It was a statement, not a question.

"It was a bequest from my father."

"My dad passed away young, too."

"My father's still alive."

Startled by his words, she lifted her gaze to his face.

"There are men who are biological fathers, then there are fathers of the heart. This is from my father of the heart."

She struggled to understand his words and their significance. "Who are you talking about?"

He cleared his throat like he was having trouble

speaking, too. "His name was Manny. He was my first boss. He taught me everything I know about gardening." He quickly changed topics, "I liked the way you handled the Crenshaws today."

"Just doing business."

"I know you weren't too enthused about residential landscaping at first."

"You were right. We have to serve all our customers, according to their needs."

Her candid admission appeared to please him. "I can hardly wait to get you using the design software. I know you'll get a real kick out of it."

A kick in the stomach. That's what it felt like now. The moment had come. They were alone and if she didn't tell him now, it would only lead to worse embarrassment later on.

She took a deep breath. "Farrell, I don't think that's going to work out for me."

"It's a great program," he countered. "Just give it a chance, and if you don't like it, we can always purchase another."

Her cheeks burned with distress. "I've never..." she said slowly, "I've never even touched a computer. I can't do it."

Chapter Five

"Really?" Farrell gave her a quizzical look.

Cat sensed his surprise. What would he think of her?

"Well, there's a first time for everything." He grinned at her. "Let's go down and see how you like it."

He was being kind, but Cat's spirits drooped lower. "Farrell, I'm only good at growing things. I was never good at school."

He ignored her protests and hustled her down the wooden steps to Laurette's cellar. Trying to stop him was like trying to stop a cold front from moving in. Useless. *Gage Farrell, you make me crazy! Why can't you ever just take no for an answer?*

She saw that Farrell had taken over half the unfinished basement as a bedroom-office. "I thought you were staying in the attic."

"The ceiling was too low. Kept bumping my

head." He led her to a desk set up against the white-painted coarse concrete wall. "Staying down here gives Laurette and Chuck more privacy, and I should be cool all summer."

She nodded, but the black laptop on the desk absorbed all her attention. It still reminded her of a big black beetle. She still wanted to squash it.

Farrell patted the back of the gray office chair invitingly. "Sit down. Before you know it, you'll be designing a garden."

Disregarding his bright tone, Cat still hung back, her panic level rising. "I already know how to design a garden with paper and a pencil. What's wrong with that?"

Her partner halted, then gazed at her searchingly as though trying to read her thoughts.

Frustration burned in her stomach. She lowered her eyes to evade his. He wasn't going to take no for an answer. Stubborn just like her father. Turning away, she wished she were anywhere but here.

Then her sense of humor kicked in. Anywhere, Cat? The Sahara Desert in July? She sighed. All right. With a noisy groan, she flopped down on the chair and glared at him. "You remind me of my fourth-grade teacher, Mrs. Taylor."

"One of your favorites, no doubt." Still watchful, he gave her a teasing grin.

Cat's mouth was dry and her palms were moist. "No. She insisted I learn long division."

"And you did, didn't you?" Farrell's light tone reassured her somehow.

This isn't brain surgery. If I can't learn it, what

can he do, fire me? She took a deep breath. "Yes, Mrs. Taylor taught me long division."

"If you learned long division, a computer will be child's play."

Cat glanced up and found her head just an inch below his square chin. His closeness nearly overwhelmed her. She fought to keep her mind clear. These intense flashes of attraction to her partner were becoming a frequent nuisance and right now a major distraction. *Get hold of yourself. Concentrate, Cat, she told herself.*

She rose slightly. "Maybe Laurette could show me tomorrow."

With his firm hands on her shoulders, he pressed her back down. The touch of his hands warmed her. "No time like the present." He sat down on a stool next to her and tapped a key on the computer. The screen flared to life with a burst of trumpet music. "Now." He picked up her hand.

A shiver worked its way up her arm. She steeled herself against the enticing sensation.

"Put your hand on the mouse. That's what you need to get started." He guided her hand to it.

Under her hand, a smooth, rounded lump of plastic; over her hand, Farrell's strong and, yes, calloused fingers. It was hard to tell which unnerved her more.

"Now, relax. There's nothing to this."

Right. I believe that. Yeah, who are you kidding, Cat?

"Look at the screen. See the arrow there? That's the cursor." His rich voice went on calm and sure, "Move the mouse. See how the arrow, called the cursor, moves as you move the mouse?'' Farrell swirled her hand and the arrow, cosmically connected to the plastic mouse, rotated in the same way.

Her stomach swirled in the same motion. She willed herself to concentrate on the screen, not Gage's hand over hers.

"See, it's easy. You're going to laugh at yourself for worrying. Now let's open programs. That's right. Move the mouse to it. Great. Now click the left side of the mouse. That's it.''

The screen brightened again with the same photo of the lush green flower garden that Cat had seen before. Its allure hadn't diminished, either. *I want to learn this.* This admission surprised and strengthened her. The clean scent of Gage's soap permeated the inches between them.

"This software is really user friendly. You may want something more advanced.''

"No.'' Cat licked her dry lips. *Don't rush me!* "Now what do I do?''

"Move the cursor up to File. Click the left button.'' He led her through setting up the file and drawing the dimensions of a patio garden for the Crenshaws. His nearness, his confidence in her, wound around her like a warm cocoon. When she slipped and made a mistake, he didn't get short with her. His patience encouraged her. She found herself smiling as she began to gain mastery in controlling the slippery movements of the cursor. *He actually believes I can do this.*

When he withdrew his hand, she turned to look at him and found his nose only centimeters from hers. All the breath leaked out of her as though someone had pushed her from behind. Her nose bumped his. Her breath caught in her throat.

"Yoo-hoo! Anybody home?" a muffled voice called from upstairs in the kitchen. "Yoo-hoo! Cat, I saw your truck in the drive!"

"I'm down here," Cat jumped up and managed to bump into Farrell's chin, nearly lose her footing and almost land in his lap. After this near miss, she ran for the steps.

The door at the top of the stairs opened. Mrs. Hansen, a member of Cat and Laurette's church, looked down at them. "Where are Chuck and Laurette? I thought she was still off her feet. Is this Chuck's friend?"

Farrell followed Cat upstairs. Flustered at being caught alone with her partner, she made the introductions. Plump and rosy, Mrs. Hansen stepped aside and let her pretty thirteen-year-old daughter, Morgan, walk to the stove and set down the casserole dish. Delicious aromas of oregano and basil wafted from it.

"More food?" Farrell asked, sounding pleasantly surprised.

Cat smiled, feeling pride in her church family's faithfulness.

"Hi, Cat!" Morgan said brightly, her eyes focused on Farrell.

"Morgan, thanks for helping your mom," Cat said with a wry grin.

"Oh, yeah." Chestnut-haired Morgan dragged her attention back to Cat. "Say, Laurette says you're

coming to our youth group's first meeting, a video
and popcorn party here in two weeks.''

Thanks for asking me first, Laurette! No, Cat hadn't
heard this from her cousin yet, but Laurette always
did things this way. And Cat understood Morgan's
eagerness for the youth group. Summer could be
deadly boring in the small town. Morgan had grown
up just down the block from Laurette and had often
followed Cat around like a little sister. As an only
child, Cat had delighted in Morgan's affection.

"Yeah, Laurette said you and Aunt Bet will have
to help out 'cause she can't move around much.''

"I guess I'll be here, then." Cat grinned ruefully.

"Great!" Morgan's curiosity had drifted back to
Farrell again.

Cat shook her head. Evidently Farrell's charm affected females of all ages. If only Morgan knew what
an aggravating man he could be. Suddenly the memory of his hand over hers as they sat at the computer
disrupted this line of thought. She swung away from
him.

"Thank you for bringing another meal,'' Farrell
said. "I'll be sure to tell Chuck and Laurette.''

"No problem.'' Mrs. Hansen beamed. "Just made
a bigger batch of what we were having. Come on
now, Morgan, let's leave them to enjoy the food.
There's plenty for you, too, Cat. Don't be shy.'' The
mother pushed her daughter out the door.

From the garage, Cat heard Mrs. Hansen say to
Morgan, "Really, staring isn't polite.''

"But, Mom, he's so handsome.''

Too true, Morgan. Cat uncovered a corner of the

casserole dish and breathed in the delicious scent. "Mrs. Hansen's lasagna. Thank you, Lord!" She glanced over her shoulder and caught Farrell staring at the door. He wore the most peculiar expression.

"Farrell?" Cat murmured. "What is it?"

He didn't answer.

Had he even heard her? His hand went to his scarred cheek.

While trying to analyze his reaction, Cat switched on the oven and slid the dish inside. She turned to him uncertainly. Was it possible he didn't realize his scars did nothing to diminish his good looks? More importantly, had Morgan unwittingly taken his mind back to the cause of his scar, the fatal boating accident? Her heart grieved for the loss of his friend. How would she survive losing Laurette? Did he somehow blame himself? She ached with sympathy, but men didn't appreciate that.

The need to stir him from this troubled mood turned her sassy. She put one hand on her hip. "So? Can you work in spite of the tantalizing aroma of lasagna or are we done with Computer Lesson One?" She would have just as soon stopped while she was ahead, but obviously Morgan's reaction to him had touched a raw nerve.

"After you, partner." He motioned toward the basement door.

Cat preceded him down the steps. She recalled his earlier mysterious comment about the "father of his heart." She'd become accustomed to Farrell's always trying to hide his limp. Were there other wounds he was hiding? Deeper ones?

* * *

Gage had never spent a Saturday night quite like this one—not even when he was thirteen. Chuck and Laurette's stuffy kitchen was standing-room-only and buzzed with voices. Like a beautiful queen on her throne, Laurette sat in a webbed, aluminum lounger giving directions and carrying on a conversation with Cat. Standing near Cat, Gage tried to act as though he felt comfortable in the midst of the four teens, all wearing jeans and T-shirts. Wearing white jean shorts which nicely revealed her healthy tan, Cat certainly appeared at ease.

Cat's tan was the real thing, not the product of a tanning salon. So far, Gage hadn't seen one of those in Eden. He had several ideas rolling around in his head for possible new businesses he might open in Eden. But a tanning salon? No. Not his style at all.

Then the new idea uppermost in his mind elbowed its way to the forefront. Would he be able to get a moment alone with Cat to bring up the new project? He didn't think she could possibly reject the opportunity, but with Cat—who knew? She still acted like turning on a computer ranked with having a root canal.

"How many more batches of popcorn will we need?" Laurette asked over the sound of popping corn.

The aroma of popcorn and the melted butter made Gage think of movie theaters. Even after a substantial supper, he couldn't stop his mouth from watering.

"About two more," Cat called back. "I'm figuring

about one paper shopping bag full for each guy and a half for each girl.''

"That's not fair!" Morgan objected. "I can eat as much as these two!" She pointed at the two boys of the group.

In return, they made faces and threw a few stray kernels of popcorn at Morgan.

"Welcome to the world of adolescents," Cat whispered into Gage's ear, then she raised her voice. "You two boys go into the living room with Mr. Farrell and move the couch so we all fit in front of the TV."

Self-consciously, Gage moved forward and his two assistants followed. They paused at the entrance to the small living room done in off-white with dark-green furniture. "Okay..." Gage combed his memory for their names. "Ryan and Phil, we need to move the sofa so it's lengthwise against that wall."

"Why?" Ryan quizzed. Freckle-faced with red hair, he looked confused.

"It looks fine to me where it is," Phil agreed. The boy needed a haircut badly, and his glasses were stuck together with duct tape. Gage's mother would have committed hari-kari before she'd let him out of the house looking like that. Evidently, Phil's mother was wise enough to expect a boy to be unconcerned about his appearance at thirteen.

"We need to move it, so there will be enough room for all of us to sit on the floor." Gage motioned both of them to go to the other end.

"Who's going to sit on the couch then?" Ryan

asked. The roll of baby fat around his middle bobbed as he walked.

"Laurette has to keep her feet up 'cause of the baby." Phil, tall and thin, looked at Gage. "Which way do you want us to move our end?"

Gage stooped and positioned his hands on the cloth underside of the couch. "Toward the TV. Okay?"

The boys grunted their understanding.

"Bend your knees and lift." Gage did the same.

Their end of the forest-green sofa rose, but wobbled unevenly. "Ry, lift your side higher," Phil whined.

The sofa leveled. Gage walked forward, the boys backward. They pivoted as they moved. "Okay, set it down easy."

Ryan let go.

"Ow! Ry!" Phil yelped. "You just missed my foot." Phil set down his side, then shoved Ryan. Ryan tripped over his own feet and bumped into the floor lamp.

Gage leaped forward. Too late. The lamp crashed to the rug.

"Hey!" Cat's voice rose over the sound of popping corn and girl giggles. "What's going on in there?"

"Just a minor mishap. No big deal." Gage picked up the lamp, righted it, and unbent the dent in the fan-shaped shade. He looked to Ryan. "Next time don't be in such a hurry."

"Sorry." Ryan turned bright red.

"Apology accepted. Now let's see if they need any help in the kitchen." How long before Chuck got back and Gage could fade into the background? Should he wait until morning to put the deal before

Cat? Maybe she wouldn't want to talk business here. Maybe it would be impossible to talk business here.

The three males weren't wanted in the kitchen and for no apparent reason, Ryan and Phil started shoving each other. Gage thought swiftly. He had to keep the boys from growing restless. "Okay—out to the drive." On his way through the garage, he snatched up the basketball. Outside, he dribbled, then tossed it at the old basketball hoop mounted above the garage door.

After it dropped through the net, Phil caught it and dribbled it away. Ryan leaped forward running between Phil and the net. Gage sighed inwardly. *Thank heaven for basketball.*

Leaving the two girls to empty and fill the popcorn popper once more, Cat watched the impromptu basketball game from the kitchen doorway to the garage. She hadn't expected Farrell to hang around after the youth group arrived that night. He hadn't seemed to be the type to be interested in thirteen-year-olds.

"He's so cool," Morgan breathed from behind Cat.

"Who?" Cat asked. "Ryan or Phil?"

"No, Mr. Farrell."

Cat grinned ruefully. Leaning against the doorjamb, she tucked her hands under her arms. "Hush. Never say that loud enough for a man to hear you. It's very bad for them."

She felt Farrell's gaze touch her. She braced herself, resisting any reaction to him. She wouldn't allow herself to act like a thirteen-year-old girl, too. How embarrassing.

Catching a whiff of scorching popcorn, she straightened up and turned back to the kitchen where Ginny, the other girl in the foursome of teens, was supposed to be watching the popcorn. "Ginny, don't let it burn! We'll never live it down!"

Within minutes, Chuck and Bet drove up, dispersing the basketball players. "Mission accomplished!" Chuck declared as he got out of the car. "Two gallons of root beer and two videos!"

Cat hung back, letting Chuck and Laurette lead the meeting. Somehow Laurette managed to get Cat and Farrell sitting side by side in the midst of teens. Was Laurette trying to matchmake? *That's all I need.*

The first video, an old horror film from the fifties, showed giant locusts taking over Chicago. The youngest generation in the room found the special effects more amusing than frightening. Laughter and loud hoots lifted Cat's mood.

She and Farrell had worked together more than six weeks now. Outwardly, they worked together easily, but underneath, Cat didn't feel comfortable yet. How was it that she possessed some type of "Farrell" radar? Whenever they were in the same room, she always seemed to keep track of him. She longed for the day she'd relax and he'd have no effect on her.

The longer she worked with him, the more questions she had about him. Why did he leave Chicago? What was he looking for in Eden? And tonight, why did he look like he was about to spring something on her? She could see the signs. He kept looking at her as if he were measuring her.

The second video, an old Disney movie, caught the

teens' interest in spite of themselves. When it ended, Chuck called the organizational part of the meeting to order. "Now as soon as school is over for the summer, this group will be having Bible studies here, every other Wednesday at 6:30 p.m.," Chuck explained. "And you will be prepared." He gave each teen a stern look. "Laurette is going to handle the Bible study because it doesn't take any legwork."

"Don't worry!" Laurette grinned. "I'll make it interesting, and we'll play games afterward."

Only Morgan appeared to take Laurette at her word.

"What're we doing for real fun?" Ginny demanded. "I don't care what my stepfather says. If this all turns out to be just another Sunday school—"

"Laurette said it would be fun," Farrell said. "I'm looking forward to it."

Ginny blushed to her hairline.

"We'll have plenty of fun," Chuck added. "Bible study every other Wednesday, games after, a fun activity one night a month and—"

"And a community project," Bet interjected. "That's my part. I set it up already. We're going to help paint the new group home, which should be ready in the fall."

"Group home?" Ryan queried.

"Yes, the church is opening a home where six Down's syndrome adults will live," Bet replied.

The four teens traded worried glances.

"Do we have to?" Ryan asked. "I never painted anything."

"Yes." Chuck sounded definite. "You're all old enough to be of some use to your community."

All four teens looked surprised at his blunt words.

"Besides," Cat said softly, "helping others can be a lot of fun and will bring longer lasting pleasure. It's better to give than receive."

"She's right," Farrell agreed.

Well, that's a first! Cat said to herself.

Farrell continued, "All of you are just the right age to begin giving. That's something I learned from an old friend when I was your age."

A shadow passed over Farrell's face. Cat wondered what was going on inside that well-shaped head?

"Okay." Morgan eyed the adults.

"Yeah, chill." Ginny twisted a piece of dark-blond hair around her finger.

"Ginny," Bet said gently. "We're icy."

This drew reluctant grins from Morgan and Phil.

Gage looked over at Cat. He had the perfect opening. Now was the time. "Cat has an opportunity to do something for her community, too."

"What?" Cat looked instantly wary.

"The Hadley estate—" he began.

"Oh, Gage, you've heard about the garden restoration at the Hadley estate!" Bet clapped her hands.

He nodded.

"Heard what?" Morgan asked.

"Yes, what?" Cat's echo sounded hollow.

She's wondering what I'm going to drop on her. Gage grinned. "The Hadley estate in town has been officially added to the National Register of Historic Homes."

"So?" Ryan asked, obviously bored.

Cat repeated his question.

"So it needs an authentic nineteenth-century garden around it." Gage leaned forward. "And Hope's Garden should do it."

Cat wrapped her arms over each other and looked mulish. "What's the catch?"

Gage glanced away. "The city has a limited budget...."

"How limited?" Cat demanded, her eyes blazing at him.

"Limited," he admitted. "That isn't important when you have a chance to do something distinctive to your hometown."

"You're old enough to 'start giving to your community,'" Ginny added in slyly.

Shaking her head and frowning, Bet tapped the girl's knee.

Cat stared at him. "We'll talk this over. In depth. Later."

Phil cleared his throat. "Cat, I mean, Ms. Simmons..." His voice cracked and he flushed with embarrassment.

"Yes," Cat coaxed gently.

"I was wondering if you need anymore help this summer." The boy couldn't look at Cat.

"Do you have any experience?" Gage asked, then mentally kicked himself. His partner wouldn't appreciate his putting his oar in.

"I always help my mom with our garden and yard." Phil glanced up.

"Why don't you come in before school is out and we'll talk about it? You'll need a work permit since you're not sixteen yet." Cat's voice was businesslike, but kind.

"Great. Thanks." His relief showed in the way his shoulders relaxed.

Gage caught Cat's attention and smiled. He took a deep breath. For the first time in a long time, he felt connected to people around him. Everything that had just been said to the teens filtered through his mind. *Lord, I'm in the right place, aren't I? Are you listening? I want to know you better—like Manny did.*

A week later on Memorial Day, Gage drove up behind Cat's white truck and parked in Eden Cemetery. Evening was approaching. The quiet cemetery bloomed with colorful ribbons and flower arrangements both silk and fresh, showing signs of the many visitors who'd come earlier while the sun was high. When Laurette had explained that the traditional holiday was still observed in Eden, Gage hadn't been able to remember ever decorating graves on Memorial Day with his family. It had just been another day off.

He glanced around and located Cat standing in the midst of the graves. She wore her dark-green gardening smock over a pale-yellow linen dress. The color made her look like an exotic flower in this setting. Evidently, decorating her parents' plots was a dress-up occasion in her mind. At her feet lay a basket of fresh flowers and flats of bedding plants.

He got out of the car and took with him the two-gallon jug for carrying water. Laurette had supplied him with this excuse for joining Cat at the cemetery. Laurette had insisted he go. She'd said softly, "I don't want Cat to be alone."

Treading carefully around the graves, he closed the distance between him and Cat. He walked quietly, not wanting to disturb her. Her head was bowed, and she might be meditating, praying. This made him feel even more awkward. Drawing near, he opened his mouth to greet her and explain why he had come.

But a sound escaped Cat—it seemed a combination of a sigh and a sob. He knew the pain behind that kind of sound all too well himself.

He looked at her profile. She was crying.

For a second, cowardice nearly carried him back to the car. But he stood his ground. Was this why Laurette had insisted he join Cat here? Not wishing to intrude on his partner's private grief, he waited silently.

She took a handkerchief out of her skirt pocket and wiped her eyes. "I'm sorry, Dad. I know you never liked to see me crying." She drew another breath. "I brought some white alyssum and Thumbelina zinnias to plant for you and some fresh-cut flowers for Mother just as you always did for her." She bent and arranged the flats of flowers around one brass marker, then turned to the other marker next to it. "Mother, after I arrange your bouquet, I'll plant your moss roses. I'm sorry I haven't been here earlier, but the nursery is booming." She reached down and lifted a dark brass vase out of the flat brass marker. She twisted it until it clicked into place.

Gage took a few steps backward, then called, "Cat!" He strode forward holding the watering jug in front of him. "Laurette said you might need this."

Cat swung around. "Why...I...what?"

"This jug." He waved it. "Where do I fill it with water?"

She pointed to a faucet jutting up from the lawn only a few yards away. "I could have managed."

"No problem." Glad to have something to occupy himself with, he reached the faucet, positioned the jug for filling, and twisted the handle. Cold water gushed out, pounding into the plastic jug. Sprinkles flew into his face.

Out of the corner of his eye, he watched Cat arrange pink roses, white lilies, glossy green ferns, and fresh lavender lilacs into the vase. The arrangement would have dazzled the most demanding customer. Evidently, Cat believed her mother deserved the best. The sweet scent of the lilies and lilacs drew him as he carried the full jug over to her. "Should I fill the vase?"

She nodded, then moved back letting him pour the water. Laying down a knee pad, she knelt by her father's grave. She took out a trowel and began loosening the soil. "Laurette made you come, didn't she?"

He considered denying the truth, but knew it would be futile. "She said she didn't want you to do this alone."

She sighed loudly. "Laurette tends to overdramatize things. I've decorated my mother's grave every year since I can remember."

But your father's grave is still new. Gage said nothing about the tears he'd seen her shed. He wished he'd thought to visit Manny's grave on the past three Memorial Days. *But I didn't know, Manny.* He almost said the words aloud.

Why did people speak to the dead at their graves? They weren't really here, only their earthly remains. That's what Manny had taught him. Gage glanced at the marker for Cat's mother. It read: Hope Johnson Simmons, Loving Wife and Mother. Under the lady's life dates, in small letters, it read: The gift of God is eternal life.

"Your mother was a Christian?"

"Yes." Cat dug a shallow furrow and began planting the alyssum border.

He didn't know what to say next. From a few remarks Laurette had made, he didn't think Cat's father had been a man of faith. So had Cat taken after her mother?

Then the sight of Cat working irritated him. In her holiday dress, she should be sitting in the shade. "Hand me your weeding fork." He held out his hand.

"You don't—"

"Hand me the fork."

She grumbled, but pulled it from her pocket and handed it to him.

He began weeding around her mother's marker.

Cat felt the awkwardness of the situation. "I'm sorry Laurette talked you into coming." She grimaced while she set the alyssum in place.

"It's my pleasure."

Cat gave a wry chuckle. Whether he meant that or

not, she realized she felt better having him here with her. She had waited until after most other mourners had come and gone because she didn't want an audience for the tears she knew threatened. But Gage's presence helped her feel less alone, less set adrift.

Gage tossed ragweed and dandelion roots to the side of the marker. "I've never done this before. My grandparents lived in two different states and died while I was very young. I think I missed something important. I see why it was really bothering Laurette not being able to come with you. I think this is a fine tradition."

Should she warn him that Laurette appeared to be taking the role of matchmaker and that might have been her cousin's true motive? No. It was best to act like she didn't have a clue. Laurette probably wouldn't be trying to push them together if she had been busy with her normal life. On bed rest, Laurette had much too much time on her hands.

"Have you decided about the Hadley bid?" Gage asked.

"You never give up, do you?" She couldn't keep the resigned amusement out of her voice. Was she getting used to the fact he never backed down?

"Well, we need to make a decision. It's due in ten days."

She cautiously hinted at her secret fear of not being good enough. "Are you sure you wouldn't like to draw the design? I'm still learning your software program."

"*Our* software. And no, you should do it. The city committee will jump at the chance to have a local person, a blood relative of the Hadleys, design the garden. Cat, they only have three months to get the grounds ready in order to be included in the new state guide of historic landmarks due out next summer. They want the grounds done for the photo in the guide.''

"I know."

"Then what's the problem?''

Cat finished planting the border, then began patting the zinnias into the dry, loose soil. Even if she disregarded her own feelings of inadequacy and just looked at this as business, didn't Farrell ever think about the fact that they might be taking on too much? "I doubt it's feasible to take on a big project, one with such a tight schedule, right now. We're stretched to our limits. This won't be a moneymaker.''

"It would be great advertising for Hope's Garden."

"And a big drain on all our time and resources. We might have to hire another person and do a lot of research. I read the prospectus. They want it to be as authentic as possible. I've never designed a nineteenth-century flower garden before!''

"I'm sure it wouldn't be difficult to find all kinds of information on vintage garden design on the Internet.''

"Farrell, you're impossible!'' She turned toward him.

Cat's expression was disgruntled. Her eyes scorched him with indignation. A smudge of dirt decorated her nose.

Suddenly Gage was caught by the urge to lean forward and kiss her.

Chapter Six

What's going on here? Gage tried to think what they'd been talking about. He couldn't. His out-of-the-blue reaction to Cat's sweet face, abundant gold-streaked hair and that ridiculous smudge on her nose had roared through him and left him reeling inside.

"Farrell, I don't know anything about the Internet!"

He grabbed this clue, the mention of the Internet, to return to the topic at hand. "The Internet isn't difficult to navigate—"

"Time. I don't have time! Why don't you grasp the facts of the situation?"

He was getting more than the facts—way more. His sudden attraction to his business partner spelled trouble in a big way. *Take it easy, Farrell.* Mixing romance into the partnership would bring an emotional dimension to every issue. That set up any partnership to make business decisions on the basis of emotion, not logic.

When he had become engaged to Daria, he had arranged to have her consult with an associate of his, so they wouldn't be working together. Business and romance made a bad combination. He looked down and automatically began pulling up encroaching tufts of grass around the brass marker. Feeling the smooth grass and gritty dirt between his fingers reassured him things hadn't changed that much. Had they?

"Farrell?"

Glancing up, he steeled himself against reacting to Cat. "You've got a smudge on your nose."

"What has that got to do with anything?" But she pulled a white handkerchief out of her pocket again and dabbed at her nose.

"Cat, I understand your concerns. I just hate to let such a great opportunity slip through our fingers." He tossed away another handful of grass.

"I realize that. But facts are facts. There are only so many hours in the day and only so much money in the budget to pay wages."

Everything she said was true. He nodded. "I'm still not ready to let this drop. There's still time."

"Why doesn't that surprise me? Your middle name should be Stubborn." Cat paused with a reluctant smile playing at the corners of her mouth.

Her soft mouth beckoned him. He looked down.

"I have prayed about this, Farrell, but so far I haven't seen anything that would change the situation."

Hearing the hesitance in her voice, he nodded. "Maybe something will come up."

She shrugged, then stood to water the bedding

plants she had just set in place. The water made a soothing trickling sound as it poured from the large jug. Something had distracted Farrell right in the middle of the discussion. But what?

A few days later, Cat stood in one of the greenhouses with Phil as she added black potting soil to a few more hanging plants to display in front. "Okay, Phil, how many hours can you work?"

"About ten a week. I'm doing a lot of yard work, too, this summer." Hands in his pockets, Phil looked at her feet, not her face.

"Cat," Hetty's voice carried over the lush green tomato and pepper plants in the full greenhouse.

Cat looked toward the just beginning-to-show, pregnant young woman. Hetty's normally cheery face looked worried. "There are some strange people out front asking for the owner."

"Strange people?" Cat repeated and waited for Hetty to explain.

Hetty just shrugged.

"Okay, then." Cat decided to finish with the planting and send the boy back home and get up front. "Phil, get the work permit at the high school, fill it out with your mom and bring it back to me Monday."

"Thanks. Great!" Phil smiled, then walked outside to his battered bike.

Cat put down her trowel and rinsed her hands in cold water at the nearby sink and dried them. She followed Hetty out to the front.

Hetty was right. Cat braced herself. These weren't the usual customers at Hope's Garden. The woman who looked to be in her middle years was tall, extremely slender, fashionably dressed in a three-piece royal-blue pants suit. She also wore a lot of chunky gold jewelry. The man with her was her counterpart, distinguished-looking with silver at his temples and wearing an expensive sport coat.

"Did you ask for the owner?" Cat asked.

"Yes," the woman replied, "where is he?"

"I am Cat Simmons. I own Hope's Garden."

"Oh, you're the partner," the woman said casually. "Where's Gage?"

The question stumped Cat. "You want Gage Farrell?"

"We are his parents," the woman said slowly as though Cat couldn't understand normal speech. "We came to see him. Where is he?"

Cat looked to Hetty. "Did Farrell get back from handling that delivery yet?"

"No—" Hetty began.

"Delivery?" Farrell's mother snapped. "Don't you have people that handle that sort of thing?"

"We all handle that sort of thing around here, Mother." Farrell spoke from behind Cat. "How good to see you."

Cat turned to see him walk from one of the greenhouses. He didn't look thrilled to see his mother. But maybe they'd just surprised him by coming unexpectedly. She knew the feeling.

"Son, good to see you." Farrell's father held out his hand.

Farrell shook his father's hand and kissed the meticulously blushed cheek his mother offered him. "What brings you two this way?" He smiled.

"Thought we'd see how you were doing," his father replied.

His mother looked Gage over with a calculating eye. "Do you all wear those same green shirts?"

"We do." Farrell stood tall. "Appropriate, don't you think?"

"But it has your name embroidered on it like some kind of tacky bowling league shirt. As the owner, couldn't you wear something in better taste?"

"It helps customers know who they can ask for help," Farrell replied evenly.

Cat couldn't figure out what was going on. What did their shirts have to do with anything? Wasn't his mother happy to see Farrell looking tanned and healthy?

His mother shook her head and heaved a pained sigh. "Waiting on customers at a gardening place! When I think of the thousands of dollars we spent on your education—"

"Hey, Gage, how's it going?" Another tall stranger slipped out of the back seat of the gold-toned luxury sedan.

"Harry!" A look of genuine gladness took over Farrell's face. He hurried forward and the two young men grabbed each other in a playful bear hug, began slapping each other on the back and grinning widely.

Cat found herself grinning, too. Harry looked too much like Farrell, not to be his brother. Except, of course, for the ponytail and gold earring.

"Didn't that thing in California work out?" Farrell led Harry to Cat.

"Of course not!" their mother snapped. "Do Harry's things ever work out?"

The comment sounded rude to Cat, but neither Harry nor Farrell acted as if they had heard it.

"Cat," Farrell said with obvious pride, "this is my brother, Harrison Farrell."

Cat held out her hand.

"Harry, this is my partner, Cat—"

"Well, just ignore us!" their mother complained.

"Mother," Farrell said, "you were busy critiquing my clothes. If you're done with that, I would love to introduce you to Cat."

The introductions were made. Farrell's mother's name was Nikki and his father was called Duke. Farrell ended by introducing Hetty and added, "Hetty is a professor at Eden College."

"Really?" Nikki's voice showed interest. "But why are you working at Gage's gardening center?"

"Summer break. Hope's Garden is a wonderful place to work." Hetty beamed.

Cat wanted to make them feel welcome. "Farrell, maybe your parents would like you to take them around and show—"

"What we really need is a decent place to stay!" Nikki interrupted. "Would you believe not one motel in this burg is AAA approved? And the places we drove by..."

Duke spoke for the second time, "We are accustomed to better, Son. I wouldn't ask your mother to stay in any of those places."

Farrell looked concerned.

"Why don't I call Aunt Fanny?" Cat offered.

"Your Aunt Fanny?" Nikki chuckled. "Do you really have an Aunt Fanny?"

"Mother," Farrell said in a low cautionary voice.

Cat ignored the rudeness in the woman's question. "Everyone calls her Aunt Fanny. She owns a beautiful Victorian home only a few blocks off the town square. She usually runs it as a bed-and-breakfast, but she had surgery earlier this year and hasn't been taking reservations. But since you're friends, she'll probably be glad to let you rent her two rooms upstairs."

Mrs. Farrell looked unconvinced.

"Is that the bed-and-breakfast on Third?" Hetty asked.

Cat nodded.

"You'll love it!" Hetty enthused. "My husband and I stayed there on our last anniversary. It's gorgeous—all authentic antiques. The decor is exquisite."

"Really?" Nikki ran an assessing eye over Cat again. "I suppose we could look at it."

Cat made the call and soon Farrell drove away in his work truck, his parents in their car following him to the bed-and-breakfast.

Hetty and Cat looked at each other. Cat didn't want to be rude and talk about Farrell's parents, but the shock had been a big one. It must have shown in her expression.

"I thought people like that only existed on TV," Hetty said in an awed voice.

Cat couldn't help nodding in agreement. Hetty's

assessment matched hers completely. Two cars drove in and both Hetty and Cat went to help customers.

As Cat talked about composting to a college professor, her mind recalled the scene that had just taken place. She had thought having the most pigheaded man in Iowa as her father had been a challenge for her. Poor Farrell.

And poor her. After Farrell's parents left Eden, she expected she'd owe Aunt Fanny big-time.

That evening after supper, Gage sat in Chuck and Laurette's living room. He'd left his parents at the bed-and-breakfast and told them he was expected to help out with the youth group tonight. The four teens and Cat lounged around on the white Berber carpet or matching plaid red-and-green chairs while Laurette, finally beginning to show her pregnancy, reclined on the forest-green sofa. Laurette was having another bad day, so though she had prepared the lesson, Cat was going to do the talking.

Holding a black Bible, Morgan read in a serious tone, "My brothers, as believers in our Lord Jesus Christ, lord of glory, you must never treat people in different ways according to their outward appearances." She passed the opened Bible to Phil.

He began reading in his reedy, sometimes cracking voice, "Suppose a rich man wearing a gold ring and fine clothes comes to your meeting and a poor man in ragged clothes comes. If you show more respect to the well dressed man..." Phil stopped abruptly. "That's where it's marked. Is that where you wanted me to stop?"

"Yes, close the Bible please." Cat looked at the young people. "Okay, tell me the end."

"What?" Ginny twisted her ash-blond hair and made a grouchy face.

Cat went on, undaunted, "What happens if you show more respect to the well-dressed man?"

Good question, Cat. Gage had been embarrassed by his mother's rude attitude toward Cat and their work shirts—of all things!

Showing subdued bewilderment, the teens looked at Cat, then at each other.

Morgan ventured in an uncertain tone, "That's not good, is it?"

With an encouraging smile, Cat nodded. "Why?"

Ginny heaved a disgusted sigh. "Why ask us? We're not the ones judging people by what they wear! Grown-ups do that." Ginny's voice switched as though mimicking someone. "Can't you keep that hair out of your face? I don't like girls wearing slacks to church, go change right now. You cut those jeans off way too short, young lady. Throw them in the rag bag." Ginny glared at Cat.

Gage recalled Laurette telling him that Ginny's mom had remarried recently and now had two sets of children to make into a new blended family. He'd bet Ginny was quoting her new stepfather. And it didn't sound like the man was building bridges. He was building walls. *Who am I to criticize? I've never been a father, not even a husband.*

"Excellent!" Cat beamed at Ginny.

Ginny looked shocked.

Gage sat up, too. He'd thought he knew where this discussion was heading.

Cat continued, "Human beings just naturally seem to choose to judge people by what is on the outside."

So what else is new? Daria certainly had been put out over his scar. Gage tried to will away rancorous thoughts from his recent past.

"Yeah," Ryan spoke up. "But Ginny's right. I asked my dad if I could get my ear pierced. And he said if I wanted another hole in my head, he'd put one in, but not in my ear."

Wondering what he would have said in a similar situation, Gage kept a straight face. "Why did you want an earring, Ryan?"

Ryan looked at him as though the question were a stupid one. "Because all the cool guys have them."

"Exactly." Cat picked up the thread, "And that's why we dress certain ways to be accepted, to be cool. Because we know people are judging us on our appearance."

"You mean," Morgan asked, "it's like a vicious cycle?"

"Vicious circle," Phil corrected.

It's just plain vicious, Gage thought.

"You're both right." Cat smiled at them. "What's the real issue in this?"

The four teens looked at her.

"Whenever we read scripture, one of the main purposes is to understand how to live our lives."

Phil chewed his bottom lip. "I know what you want us to say, but we can't do it."

"What can't you do?" Cat asked gently.

"We can't just ignore what other people are wearing and what we wear. People would think we were nuts," Phil said in an aggrieved tone.

"But that isn't what I wanted you to say." Cat looked at each teen.

"So what's your point?" Ginny gave Cat a petulant look.

Yes, Gage echoed silently, *what's your point?*

"My point is, none of us is perfect. But all of us can make a realistic attempt to judge others by *more* than just their appearance."

"We can do that." Morgan nodded.

Gage was impressed. He hadn't guessed Cat would be such an effective teacher.

Cat patted Morgan's shoulder. "Of course, you can. Any more questions?"

The teens shook their heads no.

"Okay, Chuck, get out the bingo stuff," Laurette prompted from the couch.

"You mean that's the whole study?" Ginny objected.

"Yes, that's all for tonight." Cat grinned. "Laurette writes them short and sweet."

Just the way Manny had, Gage mused.

"Yes," Laurette agreed, smiling. "Kids, help Chuck get the game out. I've got prizes."

This promise moved the teens to cooperate. They passed out the cardboard cards and round wooden markers. Soon Chuck called out, "B—9."

Gage watched his two bingo cards on the floor beside him, all too aware Cat sat across from him. Her nearness tempted him to lean out and smooth back a piece of sun-golden hair that had fallen over her face. Again he felt that new tender connection to the people in the room, especially to Cat. The phone rang. He got up and went to answer it.

"Gage, that's you, isn't it?" His mother's voice pulled him back to his dilemma—how to deal lovingly with his parents. "This bed-and-breakfast isn't as bad as I thought it might be. We have to share a bathroom with your brother, but otherwise it's fine."

"Good."

"How's that youth group meeting going?"

"Fine." He braced himself for the negative comment he knew would come.

"You know, Gage, religion is fine and good if you don't carry it too far."

"Yes, Mother." *But that isn't what Manny said.*

"Now, tomorrow we'd like you to show us around town and tell us what your plans are."

Gage didn't like the sound of that. When his mother asked what his plans were, she usually meant she was going to give him her version of his plans.

"Mother, I need to work tomorrow."

"I'm sure your partner—what was her name, Cat?—she'll understand you need to take time for your family."

Since his mother only spoke the truth, he agreed. After he hung up, he stared at the phone. *Why did you drag Dad and Harry all the way to Eden, Mother?*

The next evening, Gage drove his truck down the lane to Cat's house. His parents followed in their se-

dan. He had spent the day showing them the town
and Hope's Garden. Harry had been more interested
in the nursery, so he had stayed there after his parents
had gone back to the B-and-B to rest. Cat had invited
them all for dinner tonight along with Chuck and
Laurette.

Wary, Gage drove to the side of Cat's home as she
had instructed him. Of course, it was gracious of his
partner to invite his family, but he hadn't expected it.
He hoped his mother wouldn't be rude to Cat. He
parked, got out and waited for his parents to join him.
Tonight he would let his parents know he had to get
back to work tomorrow and that he intended to stay
in Iowa. Then maybe his mother would tell him the
reason behind their visit.

He observed his mother casting measuring glances
at the peeling siding on the house and the aged barn
farther back on the property.

"My, this is rustic," she murmured with the lift of
her eyebrows.

"The house was built by Cat's great-grandfather,"
Gage said stiffly. He hoped his mother wouldn't be
difficult tonight.

"Some things improve with age and some don't,"
his mother replied.

Since Gage had been surprised at first over the
worn condition of Cat's home, he made no further
comment. Following a stone path, he led them around
the side of the house. There he halted, dumbstruck.
He heard a tiny gasp escape his mother's throat. He
echoed it in spirit.

The front of the old farmhouse and its rear were

totally different. Cat's backyard was a garden, but the word *garden* was inadequate. Borders of fuzzy lavender ageratum, hardy wintergreen sedum, pointy hens-and-chicks curved around deep-pink peonies, beds of lavender, pink dianthus, purple Johnny-jump-ups, and white daisies. Chartreuse Chinese snowballs and veils of lacy white bridal wreath cascaded in the rear. The remnants of the lilacs fluttered in the evening breeze, sending their sweet fragrance over them.

A white, freshly painted pergola extended from the back porch steps. Lush green vines already climbed up the supports and tumbled over the beams spanning the top. Fuchsia plants hung in baskets suspended from beams. The pergola stopped just before the entrance to a large screened-in gazebo. And somewhere in the luxuriant flower garden, water from a fountain gurgled.

"This is something," his father said, obviously impressed.

His mother frowned. "Why would someone have a lovely garden like this alongside a—"

Cat's shy greeting drowned out his mother's question. Wearing a flattering yellow cotton-knit T-shirt dress, she opened the screen door and motioned them inside. Her fresh, lithe beauty suited the bower she had created.

Aware his mother would pick up on any slip, Gage made certain no flicker of his intense awareness of Cat touched his features. He followed his parents up the two steps into the gazebo. Vintage white and natural-toned wicker furniture graced the interior. Aunt Bet, wearing a blue cotton jumper, and his brother

Harry sat inside, looking comfortable and holding tumblers of iced tea. Cat introduced Aunt Bet and Gage's parents.

"Please have a seat, and won't you have a glass of iced tea?" Cat offered in a diffident tone.

"As long as it's unsweetened." Nikki sat down.

Cat looked startled. "No, I'm afraid it's the old-fashioned sweetened kind, fixed my grandmother's way from loose tea. I'm sorry. It's the only way I know how to make it."

"Then I'll just have water." Nikki smiled tightly.

"Your grandmother didn't add anything to the tea, did she?" Duke winked.

Gage cringed at his father's broad hinting that he hoped the tea had been spiked.

"Just water, ice and sugar," Cat replied with an uncertain tilt of her head.

"Tastes great, Dad." Harry held up the glass as though toasting him. Condensation on the outside of the large clear tumbler showed the welcome contrast of the iced liquid against the warm evening breeze.

"I'll have one," Duke conceded as he sat down.

From a side table, Cat served two more iced teas and a glass of water, then sat down with one tanned leg tucked under her on a wicker rocker. "I'm glad you were able to come, but I want to give Aunt Bet the credit for the dinner. She prepared most of it."

Nodding, Gage rolled the sweet tea over his tongue. Refreshing. Watching Cat rock back and forth was refreshing, too. He sensed she had no idea the captivating picture she made in her buttercup-yellow dress with the rainbow garden background.

Crossing her legs, Nikki in a teal-green silk dress took a sip from her glass.

Aunt Bet leaned forward. "The spring water on this property is some of the best in the county."

Nikki looked nonplussed. "You mean this water came right out of the ground?"

Cat looked concerned. "Don't worry. Though there is little chance of contamination, I have my spring tested yearly."

Nikki still looked sick.

"Mother," Harry said, "where do you think that fancy name-brand water you buy in bottles is from? It comes out of the ground, too."

"But tonight," Aunt Bet teased, "no extra charge!"

Nikki held her glass and gave her son a strained look.

Cat lowered her eyes as if she didn't know what to say.

"Where are Laurette and Chuck?" Gage leaned back in the roomy wicker chair.

"Laurette didn't feel up to riding out here tonight," Aunt Bet replied. "I came out to lend a hand."

Gage also thought Aunt Bet had come to even out the group. At least, Cat would have one person of her own there. He didn't blame Cat for needing backup. With his mother, he often felt that way himself.

"Laurette felt bad that she wasn't well enough to invite you for a meal," Cat said as she pushed her foot down to make her rocker move. "So far she and the baby are fine, but she just doesn't have her normal energy."

So that's why Cat invited us. He understood now.

Nikki looked around. "Your garden is lovely and so is this gazebo. Gage, Daria would love this."

Gage stilled inside. Why would his mother mention his ex-fiancée here and now?

"Yes, but Daria wouldn't want a gazebo on an Iowa farm," Harry interjected blithely.

Thankful to his brother, Gage chuckled. "I think that's safe to say."

"You two shouldn't joke about Daria." Nikki stiffened. "She was heartbroken when Gage ended the engagement—"

"I didn't break it off. Daria did!" Gage flared. A glance at Cat showed him how embarrassing this was to her. Cat looked like she wanted to retreat. How could his mother bring this up now?

"Well, you did, to all intents and purposes, when you wouldn't have that little bit of plastic surgery before the wedding. Of course, Daria wanted you to look your handsome self—"

"Mother," Gage cut off her flow of words. He'd owe Cat an apology. Obviously, his mother didn't think Cat and Bet merited politeness. His eyes warned his mother not to continue. "After the accident last year, I had all the surgeries I want to have. I still have a hip replacement facing me."

"Women!" Duke said. "A scar gives a man's face character. I bet Daria is sorry she broke up with Gage now. I don't see a line forming…."

"Dad," Gage said in a gentle, but firm tone, "I don't think we should continue talking about this now. After all, Aunt Bet and Cat don't know anything about this." *And I didn't want them to, either!*

A brief awkward pause settled over the gazebo.

Aunt Bet said smoothly, "How did you like your tour of Eden today?"

"We were pleasantly surprised," Duke responded with a cordial smile. "We had no idea there was such a local boom going on here."

Gage made himself shake off the tension his mother had caused. Cat looked relieved at the change in topic, too.

"Yes." Nikki nodded reluctantly. "There are some gorgeous homes in Paradise Hills."

"And at only a third of the price they would be in the Chicago area. I think Gage has the right idea." Duke leaned forward. "A golf course is just what's needed in Eden. If there was a course here, we'd stay a few more days."

"A golf course?" Both Nikki and Cat said in unison. Cat looked at Gage with a puzzled expression; Nikki, a shocked one.

Wishing his father hadn't brought up this topic, Gage cleared his throat. "Yes, one of our customers mentioned that it was nearly a forty-five minute drive to the nearest golf course. I have asked around, and there's a definite market here for one. I mean to look into starting—"

"But, Gage, I expected you to come back to Chicago," his mother whined. "You just came out here for a break."

Go back? No! Until he'd heard these words, he hadn't realized what a strong reaction they'd ignite inside him. He recoiled, but he tried to keep his voice unperturbed. "Mother, I don't think I'm going to go back to—"

"Why?" she demanded. "This all comes from that Manny you insisted on working for all those years. You think you can run away from your responsibilities and just be a boy working around gardens again. But this won't work!"

Feeling cornered and embarrassed, Gage opened his mouth.

Unfolding herself like a cat waking up from a nap, Cat stood up. "Aunt Bet, would you help me in the kitchen?" They left together.

Grateful for their consideration, Gage waited until they both walked into Cat's back door. "Mother, why did you bring this up? I—"

"Let's get down to business," Harry made his first contribution to the conversation. "You know our mother didn't just drive out here to visit her favorite son."

"I don't like your tone, Harry," Duke rumbled.

"Sorry, Dad, but why can't Mother just tell Gage she wants him to come back and marry Daria?"

Strained silence settled over the four of them. Gage tried not to be rude or flippant like his brother, but he had to tell the truth. "It's over between Daria and me."

"But—" his mother began.

Gage shook his head. "No."

"But— "

"No." His reply was implacable.

"Well, so much for Plan A." Harry grinned with amusement. "Now tell Gage Plan B."

Chapter Seven

The angry whirlwind had finally passed. And they'd all escaped unscathed.

Gage stood beside Cat as they watched the gleaming red taillights of his parents' car vanish down Cat's lane to the county road. Aunt Bet had preceded them to lead them back to town.

Behind Gage, the setting sun blazed red-hot. He felt its heated rays warming his back. All through his mother's melodramatic complaints, he had held his temper, but he felt like he'd been shoved through a wood chipper.

"It's going to be another hot day tomorrow." Cat turned sideways toward the sun. "My dad always said a hot sun at evening meant a hot day tomorrow."

Gage eyed her. Should he somehow apologize for his mother's causing a scene? And what would Cat say to Plan B?

"I know it's not good to stare at the sun, but when it's so orange-gold, I have to steal a glance."

"I know." He drew in a deep breath. Now was the time for an apology, but he couldn't bring himself to explain that his mother wasn't like this all the time. Harry had pushed her far past her normal level of patience. "It's late. Let's get in and do those dishes." He touched her elbow. It's soft curve just fit his hand.

"You don't have to do—"

"I want to." With his gentle grip on her elbow, he urged her forward. "Both of us have to work the same hours tomorrow. I appreciated your inviting my family to dinner." *Though my mother didn't eat much of it.* "Helping with the cleanup is the least I can do."

Also, he wasn't ready to leave her, to leave the haven of her luxuriant garden and its blessed peace.

She moved forward, but didn't pull away from him. "You're father sure liked Aunt Bet's fried chicken. But your mother was so worried. I hope it won't really upset his cholesterol level." She sounded worried.

"Don't pay attention to my mother. My dad will be fine. He will just play a few more rounds of golf this week to work it off." Reluctantly letting go of her arm, he walked beside her into her garden, her bower. Glancing down, he allowed himself to watch the rhythmic swing of her perfectly tanned legs beneath the yellow hemline. At work, he always kept his eyes at a businesslike shoulder-high level. But he wasn't at work now.

What an evening! His hip ached. His head ached. But Cat hadn't let him down. After his mother had given Cat and Bet no choice but to retreat gracefully from the family conflict, the two women had stayed in the kitchen until Gage had gone up the back steps to signal an all clear by asking if he could carry anything out for them. Without any questions, they'd let him help bring out two steaming platters of golden fried chicken, a huge bowl of creamy yellow potato salad and fresh asparagus salad—a true feast. After the conflict with his parents, he didn't have much of an appetite. But Bet and Cat's politeness had smoothed the awkward situation. As usual when his mother wanted her way, she had stirred up a lot of emotion.

His hip ached more than usual and even his scar felt tender. Were these just psychosomatic reactions? How could he love his mother and father so much and disagree with them so completely? Gage felt drained emotionally, but he had one more challenge to face tonight. What would his partner say to Plan B? He studied her profile. Her small upturned nose fit her face as though an artist had sculpted it.

"This garden is a work of art." He had to stop and massage his throbbing leg. To hide this from Cat, he paused and motioned ahead. The pinks, reds and purples accented the lush greenery. Butterflies still fluttered in and around the garden blossoms.

"A work of love." Cat smiled and folded her arms. "My father and I started working together on this after my mother died. Daddy had painted and screened in the old gazebo as his wedding gift to her. He'd promised her a garden worthy of the gazebo."

She still called her father "Daddy." From what he had heard from Bet and Laurette, Cat's father had been a gruff curmudgeon. But he had loved his wife enough to change the name of the family business to hers and to fulfill the promise of a garden even after his wife died. That spoke of real love.

Cat's parents were both gone, but she spoke of them with love; she decorated their graves and wept for them. Obviously, she still felt connected to them. He couldn't ever remember feeling in sync with his parents. He had always felt as though someone had dropped him off on their doorstep in a basket. Only with Manny had he felt linked.

With one last rub to his leg, he followed Cat up the steps of the gazebo. A petite woman, she carried herself tall with her shoulders squared and her head held high. She looked capable and strong—and she was also understanding enough to cope with unruly visitors.

His mother would never have caused a scene like she had tonight among her own friends. His mother must have thought Bet and Cat weren't important enough to show her best face. How wrong she'd been to write off these two caring women.

Cat led him into the gazebo. Without a word, he began gathering and stacking dishes. His hand grazed hers as they both reached for the same dish. Both pulled back as if they had touched fire. ''Sorry.''

''No problem.'' Unexpectedly that same attraction he'd felt on Memorial Day hit him like a shot of adrenaline. Was it because they were alone again, away from work? He didn't think that could explain it. There was just something about Cat that made him want to forget business. He concentrated on the task at hand.

After two trips to the house, they had carried everything inside. There, Cat turned on the kitchen faucet and began to run hot water into a blue plastic dishpan in the old-fashioned white porcelain sink. "Last chance to get out of it." She grinned at him as the steam rose and the frothy bubbles bubbled and bubbled.

"I'm washing." He noticed for the first time her brown eyes were the color of dark toffee. Gazing into them, he took the dish cloth she handed him and sank his hands into the basin. "Yow!" He pulled his hands out of the water and reached over to turn on the cold water handle. "I know some like it hot, but not that hot!"

"Sorry." She took a fresh cotton cloth embroidered with faded red-and-blue teapots out of the drawer and dried the first glass he handed her. He knew he had to broach the topic his parent had forced on him, but not yet.

Mesmerized by her tangible effect on him, he worked without words. He wanted nothing to interrupt this mood, this spell Cat wove around him. She hummed snatches of a hymn, "Bringing in the Sheaves," then an old rock-and-roll hit, and more. They worked together in the near silence—just the swish of the dishrag, the trickle of the water and Cat's soft soprano. The peace and the rhythm of the shared task soothed Gage's frazzled nerves. The creamy nape of her neck, so close, intrigued him.

He watched her hands as they moved—completely efficient, no lost motion. Gage's delicious consciousness of Cat spun a web around him, invisible but real.

Drawing away from temptation, Gage straightened. Glancing around the kitchen, he recalled what Cat had said to Samantha about living with four generations of antiques. Beside them, a small black antique fan oscillated slowly back and forth keeping the warm air moving. Everything in the kitchen from the round oak pedestal table and ladder-backed chairs to the glass-covered cabinets was from years past—even the silverware and china he washed. The gleam of worn, scrolled silver plate and the gilded band around each ivory plate shone among the bubbles in the dishpan and deepened the mellow mood he was being drawn into.

Get your mind on business. You have business to discuss tonight.

"This is just my everyday stuff. I didn't have time to bring out the good china and silver," Cat apologized.

He looked at her. Did he look like he was thinking about utensils? "This was perfect." It suited Cat. Everyday silver. Not stainless steel, silver plate. Bet had told him Cat lived with—and used—thousands of dollars worth of antiques daily. Maybe that was one reason why she'd showed this bond to her family.

Cat grinned suddenly. "Our good silver, the sterling, is stolen goods."

"What?" She'd startled him.

She giggled. "My great-grandmother Catherine Hadley, the banker's daughter, the one who lived in Hadley House, was unmarried and thirty. One day she drove her gig out here. This was about 1900 or so. My great-grandfather Joshua had lost his wife six months before. His mother was living with him and taking care of his two little boys.'' She paused.

''So?'' Her eyes had crinkled up with her amusement. Her lashes were thick and golder brown from the sun.

''Great-grandmother walked in and shocked Joshua's mother by taking a tour of the whole house and grounds. Then she sat down to tea. When my grandfather came in, she asked to speak to him alone.''

''Go on.'' The curling wisps of hair around her face fascinated him. They had been bleached white-blond from the sun.

''She proposed to Joshua.'' She laughed. A sunny sound which wrapped around his heart.

''She what?'' He halted with a dish in hand.

Cat nodded gleefully.

''What did your great-grandfather say?'' Gage smoothed the dishrag over another ivory china plate. He handed it to her. She took it, but he held it a fraction longer than necessary, linking them for a second.

''Joshua said her father would disown her if she married a poor dirt farmer.''

''And?'' he coaxed.

''Catherine said she didn't care. She thought they would suit each other. So to avoid opposition, two days later, they eloped to Keokuk.''

''Let me guess, she brought the silver with her.'' Gage handed her the dish. What an idea. Obviously, Cat had inherited her great-grandmother's ability to take action. What had Joshua's first reaction been to

Catherine's proposal? Shock? Or had he already been admiring Catherine Hadley from afar? Gage's heart sped up a beat or two.

"Yes, she brought all the sterling and all her late mother's jewelry. She claimed it as her inheritance. Her father was furious." Cat dried the plate, then set it on the stack of plates in the cabinet to her right.

"Did he ever forgive her?"

"No, unfortunately not." Cat fell silent.

So Gage wasn't the only one who was a disappointment to a parent. "Do you think they were happy?" He watched her closely. Cat would tell him. She never withheld the truth. Had the banker's daughter and the poor dirt farmer found happiness?

"Yes, they had five children together and both of them were highly thought of in Eden. Catherine was a suffragist and marched in front of the state capitol."

"Somehow that doesn't surprise me." Gage went on, washing and handing dishes to Cat. This evening was nearly over and he still needed to discuss Plan B with her. Though he should have thought of a smooth way to bring up the subject, nothing had come to mind. Cat, the lady herself, had kept intruding, lifting his thoughts away from business. As a salesman, he knew better than to just drop an idea on someone, but time was slipping away in the quiet kitchen. He might just as well go ahead. "I have a favor to ask you."

She looked up into Farrell's face. Did he realize his scar's redness had faded since April? Everyone only seemed to see his handsome features. Didn't they see the man whose green eyes revealed so much more? Now he looked like he was in pain. Was his leg hurting him? Or what could be so difficult to ask her? "Yes?"

Farrell's troubled expression deepened. "I know you are not going to like it, but I need to ask you."

"What?" His somber mood drew her sympathy. She took a step closer. They almost touched. His nearness had been playing havoc with her insides all evening.

He inhaled deeply, and his hands rested on the side of the plastic basin. "My brother needs a job. He just hasn't been able to settle down in one place after college."

Cat tried to read between the lines. "Is that why your parents came for a visit?" She'd sensed something was wrong.

"Partly. They're not happy with my decision to leave the Chicago area. You probably understood my mother is disappointed about the ending of my engagement to Daria, too."

She touched his wrist lightly, wordlessly asking for another item to rinse and dry. The feel of his warm skin under her fingertips made it hard to pull away.

With his chin tucked low, he began intently washing a handful of silverware, but his concentration on the chore couldn't mask his gloom.

Why had he mentioned Daria, the woman who had broken their engagement, Cat wondered? Was he regretting their breakup? Whatever kind of woman Daria might be, she had been foolish to push Farrell away over something like a scar. Did she think men like Gage grew on trees? Cat wanted to touch his shoulder, tell him how sorry she was he'd been hurt. She couldn't. They were only business partners, and this intimacy she was feeling had nothing to do with business.

"My brother and parents don't get along." His voice was moody, a tone she'd never heard from him before. "They wanted him to get a degree in banking—"

Cat couldn't stop herself. The idea of Harry with his ponytail and earring as a banker forced her to laugh. "I don't see Harry as a banker!"

"No." Gage half smiled at her. "He has two fine arts degrees."

Cat shook her head. "He's your renegade. He probably would have gotten along well with my great-grandmother."

"Probably." He handed her the silverware, and his voice deepened. "I was thinking he might be the answer to our problem of extra help for the Hadley bid."

His low voice had activated little jumps and skips in her stomach. Cat looked into his pine-green eyes, then looked down at the dark-red paint on the wood floor. She stopped rinsing the silverware and turned this idea about his brother over her mind. "Is your brother a hard worker?"

"If he's doing something he likes." Gage appeared relieved at this question. "He likes landscaping, and he also knows how to garden and how to research on the Internet. You would still design the garden for Hadley, oversee the project, but he could do the other work."

"I see." She began drying the silverware, working the soft cloth with her thumbs over the bowl of each spoon, the blade of each knife. "But how can we afford another full-time worker?" She knew to a penny what she needed to meet their obligations, especially making payments to Gage according to the terms of the partnership. She stood so close, his breath feathered the short hair above her ear, tickling her. She ignored a shiver up her spine.

"Harry would work for minimum wage, and he won't be full-time. He's already worked out a deal with Fanny. He gets free room and breakfast in return for doing some maintenance work. And she has an old bike he can use to get around town."

"It sounds like he wants to stay in Eden." She didn't blame him. Working for minimum wage in Eden would be preferable to living with his mother, who couldn't see Harry would never fit the life she wanted for him.

"He said something about the art department at Eden College...."

"It's the college's pride and joy." Cat put each piece of silver where it belonged in the drawer beside her. Metal on metal sounded a steady *chink-chink*. Concentrating on the task lessened Gage's sway over her. *Well, at least, it might.*

"I hadn't realized the college's art department had such a good reputation."

Cat nodded. "That's one of the reasons the college cooperated with the town to get the Hadley House on the National Register. The college's yearly art show wanted a more distinctive setting."

"Really?" He handed her another handful of silverware. "What do you think?"

She thought they'd been alone together too long tonight. She painstakingly began drying the last of the flatware one by one. She felt Gage's attention on her. This only rattled her more. *Keep your mind on the subject, Cat.* But in the end, only one answer could be given. This wasn't just business. This was family. She couldn't say no to Gage's only brother. They'd scrape by somehow. "All right. I think we will go ahead and take this as a step of faith."

"Step of faith?" He looked directly into her eyes.

She returned his gaze, standing straight in spite of her fatigue and his sway over her. "I've been praying that something would happen to make it possible to make a bid on the Hadley House and your brother's arrival has done that. We may not make a profit, but the money earned will cover our expenses. We'll let Phil work with Harry, too, so your brother won't have to do it all alone."

"Great! Thank you." He reached for her hand to shake it, but instead he caught her free left hand with its palm up. Cat's hand wasn't soft and pampered like Daria's had been. Cat's palm bore the marks of the hard work she did each day. His thumb moved over it in an unplanned caress. The desire to press his lips down onto her palm rippled through him. He glanced to her face mere inches away.

The space between them became charged with awareness. He took a step closer. Her head tilted invitingly. He bent forward to claim her soft mouth.

The phone rang.

Gage jerked upright.

Cat spun away and reached for the black wall phone. Then she handed it to him. "It's your brother." She wouldn't meet his eyes, and he didn't blame her.

Two busy days had passed since Gage and Cat had agreed to go ahead with the Hadley estate bid. The first day, Harry had camped out all day and night in Gage's office in Chuck's basement. Even while Gage slept with a pillow over his eyes, Harry, online, had harvested information on Victorian garden design and on nurseries that stocked some of the rare vintage shrubs and flowers. The second day, Gage and Cat had taken turns helping measure the site itself, which included a tour inside and outside the Hadley estate. The grounds covered a full city block just down from the town square.

Now Gage, Cat and Harry sat around Cat's round, old oak kitchen table, hovering over the computer. Cat and Harry worked together planning the design. Gage, beside him with a calculator and price sheets, which Harry had printed out earlier, kept the running tally on costs. As the three of them worked together, a way to make this project easier on Hope's Garden's finances had occurred to Gage. But could he get Cat to agree?

Once more in Cat's cozy kitchen, he recalled vividly what happened two nights ago. Cat and he had washed dishes together in this kitchen, and he had nearly kissed her. That near kiss had been a close call.

It would have been out of line to kiss Cat when he had no intention of pursuing a relationship with her. After Daria, he had no thought of taking another chance on love anytime soon—especially not with his business partner.

Frankly, he couldn't even remember why he'd become engaged to Daria. But they'd been thrown together in their careers and socially until they'd become a couple. He and Daria had grown up in the same neighborhood, gone to the same schools. She'd understood his life. What she hadn't understood was Gage hadn't settled on their shared life-style for good. The accident had ripped away the smooth husk of his life, and he came away changed. He and Daria had no longer been a match.

"Harry, I can't believe you got this all together in just one day." Cat lifted the stack of pages beside the laptop.

Gage kept his face toward the calculator to hide his smile. He wanted to say, "I told you so." Cat had done a complete one-eighty about computers and the Internet. He had known she could do it. Satisfaction expanded inside him. He also wanted to say, "I'm proud of you," but he couldn't say that, either.

Harry kept his eye on the screen and his hand on the mouse. "I could have gotten more. There are tons of gardening and Victoriana sites on the Web. Now, Gage, we need you to run the figures for the rose garden that's just off the side veranda."

"Okay." Gage flipped through his stack of pages. "How many did you need?"

Harry looked up, his face serious. "Two dozen.

Various colors. Make sure they're marked vintage. No new hybrids.''

Gage nodded. He was glad his brother was here. He enjoyed the way Harry had taken on the project wholeheartedly. But he didn't like Cat sitting so close to his brother. Harry liked to flirt with pretty women.

In an unusual, clipped businesslike tone, Harry asked, "Now, Cat, for the herbaceous border, do you have enough ageratum, alyssum, begonias, coleus, scented geraniums, petunias and zinnias in stock?"

"Everything, but the scented geraniums," Cat murmured.

She hovered around Harry. Gage clenched his jaw. She didn't have to hang over the computer and Harry like that.

Harry pointed at his brother.

"Right." Gage nodded belatedly. "Vintage scented geraniums. How many?"

"Three dozen." Harry turned the screen, so Cat could see the design better. "How's that?"

Cat's answer was drowned out by the ringing of the phone. She answered it, "Hello, Mrs. High. How can I help you?"

A pause.

"Yes, we are making a bid on the Hadley estate. But we might not get the project. It all depends on which bid and design the commission prefers." After a few more pleasantries, Cat hung up.

Gage gave her a questioning look.

Cat propped her hand on the back of Gage's chair and leaned toward him. "Phil told his mother he might be helping out on the Hadley estate."

"Didn't she want him to?" Gage asked. Reveling in her nearness, he studied her freckles, tiny dots of gold, on her arm.

"No, she was thrilled."

"Phil's a good kid," Harry said from behind the laptop. "Said he'd work extra for free. Seemed to think the Hadley estate was a big deal."

"Really?" Gage turned off the calculator. The overhead lamp highlighted the natural blond in Cat's hair making it appear interlaced with spun twenty-four-carat gold.

Cat let go of Gage's chair and resting her forearms on the ladder-backed chair, leaned farther forward. The curve of her neck drew his attention to her soft, rounded earlobe. "This project has turned into something good for Eden. I mean, *more* than we first thought," Cat said seriously. "This is a way for the three different groups in town to work on something together for the good of the whole community."

"How do you mean?" Gage asked, very aware of the light fragrance coming from Cat's hair. He didn't think she wore cologne, but her shampoo must have been some enticing blend of herbs and flowers. These flashes of attraction to her came with more frequency each day. Stick to business, he told himself.

Cat bit her bottom lip as she frowned. "I'll try to explain. Before the new people came—"

"You mean the new people attracted by the Venture Corporation software firm?" Gage asked.

From pressure, her lower lip flushed rosy. She nodded. "Before, there were just two groups; the townies like me and the college people like Hetty."

"And never the twain shall meet?" Gage grinned approving the change in Cat toward the newcomers. He'd seen firsthand how customers like Samantha and Dex no longer intimidated her.

"Something like that." She smiled back at him. "But the new group moving in kind of shook things loose. Now the townies want to spruce things up in the older part of town—"

"To look better in comparison to the yuppie Paradise Hills?" With raised eyebrows, Harry glanced at them over the laptop screen.

Scraping it on the hardwood floor, Cat pulled a chair out and sat down within inches of Gage—suddenly much too close for his comfort. He drew in a ragged breath and studied the row of numbers in front of him.

She answered, "That may be part of it. Anyway, Eden is taking new pride in itself and really wants to be in that state guide next year."

"I know," Gage said as he continued concentrating on his task. "And I want our nursery to be cited as the designer and supplier of the Victorian garden."

Cat gave him a provocative grin. "I keep thinking that great-grandmother Catherine would have a good laugh over this."

"Why?" Gage asked.

A teasing glint danced in her dark toffee eyes. Cat wrinkled her nose. "Because the Hadleys have died out and the Simmons have flourished."

"What? I don't get it." Harry looked up.

Gage stretched, his neck and shoulders had tightened. He stood to put some distance between himself and his attractive partner. "Cat is a descendant of the Hadleys—"

"Yes, the one and only renegade Hadley," Cat interjected.

"Catherine Hadley?" Harry asked. "You're her namesake?"

"Yes."

"Then why do you go by Cat?" His hand on the mouse stilled.

She looked surprised. "My dad called me that when I was a little girl—"

"You're not a little girl anymore. I will henceforth call you Catherine." Harry made a motion as though knighting her.

"But I've always been Cat."

"Maybe you need to change along with Eden."

Gage studied her. Harry had put his finger on something. "Cat" didn't suit his partner anymore.

Halting this line of thought, he shifted gears mentally once more. *Back to business.* Now was the time to try to persuade her. He hoped he wouldn't wound her pride. "Cat..." He couldn't bring himself to say her full name though the idea attracted him. It would sound...

Back to business—now! Make the suggestion! "I know this project is really going to cut into our nursery stock budget, so I want you to delay the next partnership payment to me, maybe even the next two—"

"No!" Cat put her hands on her hips. "I, we won't need to do that."

"But—"

She hopped up, her eyes flashing. "No, you'll need that money to get your golf course started."

He hadn't even suspected she'd taken his golf course plan seriously. "Do you think it's a good idea?" Gage's voice came out funny, reminding him of Phil's changing voice. He held his breath waiting for her judgment. If Cat didn't think it was a good idea, he'd have to reconsider.

"I do." She nodded her head once as though deciding the matter. "Have you done anything beyond talking to people?"

He cleared his throat. "I've started driving around looking at large parcels of land."

"So, big brother, you plan to settle down in Eden?" Scraping his chair back, Harry stood up, stretching toward the ceiling, then touched his toes.

"Yes, what do you think?"

"I think it was good that you broke up with Daria when you did." Harry smirked. "I have a hard time picturing her here. Anyway, I might hang around for a while myself. Maybe there is room for a new fourth group—out-of-work artists who want to drive their mothers crazy."

Cat paid no attention to the two brothers as they bantered about Harry's bad joke. Had Gage been thinking about those moments of closeness they shared two nights ago in this very kitchen? *I hope not.* Thinking of them warmed her, but it had been just one of those crazy moments in life.

Meeting Gage's parents had been an eye-opener for her. Trying to imagine her father and Gage's parents in the same room was mind-bending. Of course, that could never happen, but it demonstrated the gulf between Gage and herself. They were from two totally different worlds.

Three weeks later, Cat parked in the drive of the future group home, a modest raised ranch. She opened her cell phone and speed-dialed Hope's Garden.

Harry picked up.

"Did they call yet?" Cat couldn't keep the urgency out of her voice.

"No, are you at the group home?"

"Yes."

"Okay. We'll call as soon as we hear anything. Why are you worrying? It's in the bag. Our design will blow the bloomers off any other bid."

Cat grinned at Harry's colorful language. "All right. I just didn't expect nurseries from as far away as Des Moines to put bids in, too."

"Don't worry. Be happy," Harry teased in a singsong voice.

Cat wished she'd gotten Gage. Cat had more confidence in Gage's opinions. But, of course, she couldn't say that to Harry.

"I know you would rather hear it from my brother—"

"Stop." Cat laughed. "Call me—whenever." And she snapped the phone shut.

Lord, I really want this job. Help me take the commission's decision calmly if we don't get it. But I really want it!

Cat got out of her truck and joined Aunt Bet with

the four teens as they stood in front of the house. Someone had started to paint the window frames white, but must have been called away. Cat made a mental note to bring flowers over for a small bed beside the door; or maybe a planter would be easier for the new residents to take care of. And the lawn needed cutting and fertilizing.

She turned her attention to the group. Everyone had worn grubs to paint in. She asked, "How many of you have painted before?"

Phil raised his hand.

Cat had expected inexperience. "Okay. Then I'll have to show each of you how to do the necessary jobs."

"What's the big deal about painting?" Ginny gave Cat a sullen look. "You put the brush in the paint and then slap it on the wall."

"Wrong. We won't be using brushes. We'll be using foam painters and rollers. Only really skilled house painters use brushes." Cat returned a bright smile for Ginny's glare. "Anyway, first the interior baseboard and trim have to be scrubbed so the masking tape will stick. Next comes masking the trim with tape to keep paint off it. Then the walls must be edged and finally we paint."

"How long are we going to be here?" Morgan looked worried. "I have to baby-sit tonight."

Aunt Bet looked at a clipboard she held. "Today, we've been given the dining room to paint, and we're supposed to prepare the downstairs bedroom for painting."

"I don't want to do any of that scrubbing," Ryan complained.

"Me, neither," Ginny agreed.

"Everyone is going to do every job." Aunt Bet looked at them over half glasses.

"Right," Cat seconded. "That way no one can complain."

"Or, at least—" Bet grinned "—everyone will have equal complaining rights."

Cat chuckled. The four teens displayed a variety of unhappy faces—Phil, resigned; Ryan, disgruntled; Morgan, philosophical; and Ginny, rebellious.

"Why aren't Chuck, Laurette and Gage here to help?" Ginny demanded.

This made Cat think of calling Hope's Garden again. She pushed this thought aside. *A watched pot never boils.*

"Cat and I are perfectly capable of showing you what to do." Bet looked at Cat, her expression brimming with amusement. "How about I take Ryan and Ginny to prepare the dining room since they *can't wait* to start scrubbing. You help Phil and Morgan start painting. We'll work a half hour and switch."

Cat agreed, and they all trooped into the two-story house undergoing renovation. Tarps on the carpeting, ladders, sawhorses and a row of gallon paint cans testified to ongoing work.

In the dining room, Cat demonstrated how to use an edging tool and how to paint a wall with a roller. Phil took the long-handled edger and began carefully running the pale-yellow paint along the premasked trim. Cat helped Morgan learn how much paint to keep on her roller, then showed her the way to roll the paint on smoothly. As soon as Phil had edged one wall, Cat and Morgan began at opposite ends of it intending to meet in the middle. Soon, the sound of the rollers in motion, that rhythmic pulling-tape hiss, was heard.

In the other room, Bet turned the radio to an oldies station and soon a song about a girl falling in love filled the house. Smells of pine cleaner and latex paint mingled and floated around them.

Morgan glanced shyly at Cat. "Are you and Gage dating?"

Cat pushed too hard on the roller. Paint streaked down the wall. With her roller, she caught it and smoothed it out. "We're just business partners." But the words of the song made her think of Gage. He was fine in so many ways. *Don't go there, Cat.*

Morgan gave her an I-know-better look. "Everybody knows his parents came to visit, and he is always with you. It would be so cool if you two fell in love."

Eden Gossip Central had obviously been keeping close watch over Cat. She tried not to let it get to her, but it still rankled. "His parents visited him. We work together. That's it."

Suppressing a grin, Morgan looked unconvinced.

The half-hour mark came, and the groups switched. After a brief demonstration, Ryan took over edging from Phil and Ginny took Morgan's roller.

The front door opened. Footsteps and voices sounded in the entry way.

"Who's here?" Ryan swung around unexpectedly.

His long-handled edger swiped Ginny's cheek with yellow paint.

The girl gasped. "Dork!" She pushed her roller into Ryan's midsection and rolled it upward.

"Dorkette!" Ryan bellowed and brought his edger down on Ginny's hair.

"Stop that!" Cat swung her roller between them like a sword. "That's enough!"

Both teens glared at each other, but halted.

"Good afternoon, Catherine."

Looking around, Cat groaned inside. The silver-haired senior pastor, Mr. Conkling, from their church looked back at her with a benign smile and an amused glint in his eye.

Cat blushed. "Sorry, pastor, things just got a little out of hand...."

"No need to explain. Youthful high spirits. You had them once, too. Catherine, I'd like you to meet two of the people who will be living here this fall and their parents."

Embarrassed, Cat would have preferred hiding in a closet. But she gave both her teens warning looks, then walked toward the strangers. "Hello, we're so glad you will be coming to live in Eden."

"Hi," one of the Down's syndrome adults, a husky young man, responded, "I'm Kevin. Why do they have paint on them?"

Cat nearly answered for her teens, then halted. "Ginny and Ryan, why don't you answer Kevin?"

Ryan wore a wide streak of yellow from his waistband to his neck. Yellow paint dripped down Ginny's forehead and cheek. The two teens, both red-faced, looked at each other with hostility, then at Kevin. Their expressions softened. Finally, Ryan spoke up, "We were goofing off."

Ginny nodded in agreement.

The other future resident, a plump young woman, asked, "Doesn't it feel gooey?"

Cat grinned.

Ryan smiled reluctantly, "Yeah, we'll have to wash it off."

The plump girl stared at the wall. "I like this color. It's like sunshine."

"It is indeed," Mr. Conkling agreed. "Catherine, we'll leave you and your helpers to the painting." He led the group away.

Cat looked at the teens. "Ginny, go into the kitchen and wash yourself as best you can and don't leave paint in the sink. Ryan, you go to the downstairs bathroom and do the same."

Ryan lay down the edger. "Aren't you going to yell at us?"

"No, I think you both did such a good job of embarrassing yourselves that you won't pull something like this again. Experience is the best teacher, my dad always said. Go on. There are paper towels beside both sinks."

Still maintaining a wide berth between each other, the teens exited.

Cat's cell phone rang. She automatically reached for it, then stopped. Would this be the call about the bid?

Chapter Eight

Quietly elated, Gage sat back in the wicker chair in Cat's gazebo. To celebrate the acceptance of their Hadley bid, Cat had invited Harry, Phil, Hetty and her husband and Gage to come out immediately after Hope's Garden closed. Hetty and her husband had brought a young friend, Jo. And anytime now, Bet, Chuck and Laurette were expected. Though mostly still on bed rest, Laurette had insisted on coming.

"It's so exciting!" Hetty exclaimed. "This is a once-in-a-lifetime project." Hetty's quiet, bearded husband sat beside her looking cheerful, but content to let his wife express her exuberance.

Cat glowed with delight. She sat in the same rocker she had on the evening Gage's parents had visited. Cat had changed from her work clothing. She wore a pale-pink cotton dress with a high waist, but her tanned legs were bare and she had slipped off her sandals. As was her way, she had folded one leg up under her.

Gage thought of Daria and the contrast between her and Cat. Daria had always kept herself, her impeccable chic, together. This had been one of the first things that had impressed him about her. Daria could step out of the pouring rain and look dry and together. Would Daria ever mix bare feet with a dress? No. To Daria, bare feet only went with a swimsuit.

But why was he comparing the two women? Was it because he was on the rebound and more susceptible? Could that explain his sudden flashes of attraction to his partner?

Three months had come and gone since April first, the day he'd begun working with Cat. Only three weeks had passed since his parents had gone and Hope's Garden had put in the sealed bid for the Hadley restoration. A short time, but big changes. He felt like a different man.

"Most of the credit goes to Harry." Cat lifted her tumbler of iced tea to him. Gage focused on her dainty wrists and slender arms, so deceptively soft and feminine, but they could lift hefty bags and garden for hours without stopping.

"Not so!" Wearing tattered jeans, T-shirt and sandals, Harry sat sprawled on the dark-green painted wood floor of the gazebo, his back against one of the posts. Beside him, Hetty's friend, Jo, also in tattered jeans sat Indian style. "I just did the research and assisted Cat. She did the design!"

"But I could never have done the research as efficiently or the designing if Gage hadn't insisted that I learn to use the computer," Cat countered.

"Let's face it!" Harry grinned. "All of us are brilliant, talented and highly efficient."

Along with everyone else, Gage laughed. Cat's delight lifted her face, gave it special attraction.

"When do we start working?" Phil asked, then reddened. Gage understood the boy's bashfulness.

Harry looked to Cat, "Catherine, I plan to start tomorrow after breakfast."

Gage had come to envy his brother's easy use of Cat's real name. If Gage tried to use it, would it give the wrong impression?

She nodded. "We'll need to meet with the tree-removal company first."

Gage watched Cat as she easily discussed removal of dead trees and shrubs with Harry. He couldn't remember seeing his brother this happy in a long time.

"Food delivery!" Bet shouted coming around the corner of the house.

Gage stood up and opened the door of the gazebo.

"Did you get the steaks?" Cat came to stand beside Gage. He breathed in her distinctive fragrance of herbs and blossoms.

Chuck carried Laurette into the gazebo while Bet followed with a large brown shopping bag in her arms. Chuck settled Laurette on a wicker chaise longue, and Gage lifted the heavy bag out of Bet's arms.

"That's my contribution. I bought four huge sirloins and had them cut into steaks." Bet went to the side table where she poured three glasses of iced tea. She kept one and handed the other two to Chuck and Laurette.

"Laurette, are you sure you were up to coming out here?" Cat asked, deep concern in his voice.

"I'm feeling great. I even walked out and sat on the front porch today. I just can't stand lying around anymore! My baby quilt is almost done, and I want to get out and weed my flower garden."

"Morgan's doing that for you," Cat said.

"I know, but I'm tired of being useless!"

"You're not useless, sweetheart!" Chuck kissed her.

Gage had watched Laurette's restlessness rise over the past two weeks. Chuck worried that she got up when no one was around. After Aunt Bet introduced Hetty to Laurette, the two pregnant women began a conversation about breast-feeding.

Not a topic Gage had much interest in. "Let's take the meat into the kitchen," he said close to Cat's ear.

She nodded and brushed past him. Inside the neat kitchen, she brought out a large china platter. Keeping his mind on the task at hand, Gage unwrapped the meat and put the steaks on it while she got out long-handled cooking utensils. Then she led him to the brick grill at the rear of the garden.

The coals gleamed red-hot under the metal rack. Heat rose in transparent waves about it. Baking potatoes wrapped in foil nestled in the bed of the fire. While Cat turned the potatoes with tongs, Gage carefully arranged each steak onto the grill.

"I'm so hungry," Cat confided. "I couldn't eat today. Too nervous."

"I am proud of you." He almost added, "Catherine."

"For going hungry?" She slanted a smile up at him.

Her joy overflowed his cup. He wished he could open his mouth wide, laugh out loud, then dance Cat around the yard. With restraint, he allowed himself a huge smile. "No, for meeting the challenge of learning how to use the design software and for taking a chance on my brother."

"Not a chance—a step of faith. Remember? We still have a ways to go, but I think your brother will do a great job." She paused and looked shyly down at her bare feet. "Maybe you would like to call your parents and tell them the good news?"

Leave it to Cat to have such a kind thought. "That's very nice of you, but I don't think my parents would grasp the importance of this."

She kept her golden-streaked head bent, so he couldn't read her expression. He glanced downward, too, and glimpsed Cat's tiny feet in the green grass.

"Maybe," she began haltingly, "you should keep giving your parents chances to understand you and your brother. I know I always felt I couldn't measure up to my dad's standards. Now I understand a little more of his struggle to raise a daughter alone. I wish we had been given more time together."

Intensely aware of her, Gage focused on the steaks browning over the fire, savoring the succulent aroma of hot beef while he thought about her words. But that same old sensation of distance from his parents cropped up inside him. "I don't think my parents have ever understood Harry's need to express himself creatively."

"Maybe they just don't know what that feels like." She motioned toward the garden. "Before she died, my mother planned out this garden. My father followed her plan. When I was in fourth grade, I started scribbling garden designs on the margins of school papers. That pleased my dad, but not my teachers." Her eyes crinkled with laughter. "Dad said I had my mother's gift. Maybe your parents just don't have it." Cat's face tilted upward with an earnest expression.

Had his parents ever tried to understand Harry?

"I think your mother is afraid of losing you—of losing both of her sons."

Gage considered this. "Possibly." He glanced at the gazebo. "This project could be the turning point for Harry. A chance for him to create something solid."

"I know. It's good for Hope's Garden, too. Did you realize this opens a whole new vein of business to us?" She wrinkled her lightly freckled nose at him.

He gave her a knowing smile. "Really? You don't say?"

Cat punched his arm. "I'll never believe that dumb act so don't try it. As soon as we finish this, you will have something different up your sleeve."

To tease her, he looked up the sleeve of his green work shirt. "No! Nothing there!"

"Stop that!" She tugged his shirt.

Gage reached out and pulled her ponytail.

"You two," Chuck shouted from the gazebo, "concentrate on those steaks! I don't want my Iowa prime corn-fed beef burned!"

Cat turned bright red.

Thanks, Chuck, Gage groused.

Before long, everyone filled a plate. They sat around eating, joking. Evening shaded the sky lavender, then deep purple. The neon-green lightning bugs flashed and darted around the gazebo. Cat closed her eyes, listening to the hum of voices around her. *Life is good, Lord. Thank you for making this Hadley project possible. Please help us do a good job.*

She glanced around at the assortment of friends relaxing in the gazebo and smiled. Hetty had never been able to adapt herself to the Hope's Garden work shirt and shorts. She wore a gauzy, multicolored sundress and dangling earrings. Her friend, Jo, with blond hair so short it could be called a buzz cut, had at least five gold loops in one ear. Aunt Bet wore jeans and a T-shirt that read, Quilters Have Many Layers. A varied, but very happy group gathered in the old gazebo.

Her gaze lingered on her partner. He still remained a mystery. Why did his voice soften when he spoke of his old boss, Manny? Did he still care about the fiancée who'd broken up with him? He'd let his black-walnut-colored hair grow a bit longer. It touched the back of his collar. She imagined running her fingers through its silky texture. Her breath caught in her throat.

"Chuck?" The note of concern in Laurette's voice grabbed Cat's attention.

The voices stilled.

"What?" Chuck was already on his feet.

"I think I just had a contraction."

Chuck moved instantly into action. "Cat, call the hospital. Tell them I'm bringing Laurette in!"

After spending most of the night sitting beside her phone, the next morning Cat glanced down, bleary-eyed, at her desk at the nursery. The list of duties she had to take care of today looked overwhelming and she had no heart, no enthusiasm. *Oh, Lord, protect Laurette's baby. Please.*

She'd prayed this same prayer all night long. Chuck had finally called near dawn and said the irregular, faint contractions had stopped, but Laurette would remain in the hospital for another twenty-four hours at least. The doctor wanted to be sure the crisis had passed.

Chuck had tried to sound hopeful. The baby couldn't come this early and survive without serious complications to the child. *Lord, give the baby time. Please keep the contractions from starting again.*

Sighing, she picked up a note written in Gage's large scrawl: "Gone to deliver stock to Myer."

"No," Cat said out loud. She had wanted to do that delivery herself. Myer, a local contractor, was a sticky customer. Why was it that some days nothing went easy?

"Morning." Hetty's voice floated inside. "I brought Jo with me."

Cat recognized Hetty's friend, who Harry had kept his eye on throughout the gazebo celebration. Cat recalled that Hetty had mentioned Jo, an art major, made something they could sell at the nursery. "Hello, did you bring some of your work?"

"Yes." Jo looked eager, but nervous.

"Outside?"

The young woman nodded.

Cat cast one more worried look at Gage's note, then she followed them outside. Beside Hetty's small foreign car, the young artist had stacked a collection of copper images mounted on narrow three-foot-high poles. "Why don't you bring them out and display them in front of the plants, so we can see how they would look in gardens?"

Jo arranged the bright copper images—a sunflower, a pair of robins, a row of birdhouses, a penguin, a stylized man in tuxedo and sporting a monocle, among the plants. In spite of her fatigue and worry, Cat recognized their quality. "These are wonderful!"

"Do you really like them?" Jo asked, looking doubtful.

"Yes! I want the man in a tuxedo for my garden. What a hoot!"

Jo grinned and blushed.

Hetty put an arm around the young artist. "I told you, didn't I? She was so afraid you wouldn't like them. Now she can make money to continue her serious sculpture."

"I love them. How many do you have?"

Jo said, "It's Hetty's idea. I've made just these six designs, but I can make more."

"Let's go in and write up and sign a consignment agreement. They will sell like crazy." Cat made her voice enthusiastic though she still felt flat and teary inside.

Cat was bidding Jo goodbye when Gage drove in.

She went to meet him. Gage looked as though he hadn't slept at all—gray smudges under his eyes from lack of sleep. *I must look dragged out, too.* But she didn't care. She brought her mind back to the topic at hand. "You did the Myer delivery?"

"Right." He opened the white delivery truck door and got down. "I arrived early and decided to get it done for you. You didn't get much sleep last night either, I see."

For just a second, Cat nearly leaned her face into Gage's chest for comfort. Fighting this, she nodded. "Did you remember to get payment upon delivery?"

"Yes, you mentioned that in passing last night."

She held out her hand, struggling against the urge to take comfort from touching Gage.

From his pocket, he drew a check.

She took the check and frowned. "Darn."

"What's wrong?"

"I was afraid he would try to palm a check off on you." Her somber mood took a nose dive. *Not today, Lord. I'm just not up to this.*

"Afraid?"

"You couldn't have known," she said in a weary voice. "We never take checks from Myer. He always operates on the edge."

"The job looked pretty substantial—"

"Well, he might have the money this time," she conceded. She turned and walked to the office with Gage at her heels. Inside, she dialed the bank. "Hello, give me bookkeeping please." Pause. "Hi, this is Cat Simmons. Would you please check Myer's account number 05213 and see if there is enough to cover a

check for over a thousand dollars?'' A pause. "Thank
you.'' She looked up at Gage. "He has just closed
that account."

Gage groaned and ran his hands through his hair.
"A bad debt."

Cat stared at the check. Her mood hit rock bottom.
Tears welled up inside her. She had no stamina today.
"A truckload of shrubs and trees, right?"

He nodded. "I'm sorry. He said he had done business with your family for years."

"Only cash business." She had no choice. "Okay.
I'll go back with you. This will put us behind schedule, but that can't be helped.'' She came around the
desk.

Gage caught her arm. "You don't mean to go back
there and reload the stock, do you?"

Startled, she halted. His fingers electrified her arm.
She made herself pull away. "Of course, I do. Hetty
can take care of things here."

"All companies carry bad debts. We'll just take it
off our taxes."

She stared at him. "We don't do business that
way," she spaced her words out evenly. "I have
never cheated anyone out of a dime, and I won't allow myself to be cheated, either. What kind of business reputation do you want to have in this town?
Don't think this won't be a mark against you. It will."

"What do you mean?"

"This is a small county. If you intend to go ahead
with that golf course, you'd better not be seen as an
easy mark. And Myer is just the man to let it be
known."

He made a sound of disgust. "I hadn't thought of that. Okay. Let's go."

She handed him the check, careful not to brush fingertips. Why did she feel vulnerable today? Distance, she needed distance or she'd collapse into his arms and embarrass them both. "You'll do all the talking. Give him back the check. Tell him you weren't aware that Hope's Garden only deals in cash with him." She kept her eyes lowered. "Tell him we want cash or we reload the stuff. If he argues, give me the signal and we'll start loading."

He nodded, his face drooping with disgust.

Of all the days to have to deal with Myer. She felt like dumping a bucket of cold water over the man. How dare he try to cheat Gage! And today of all days! She marched out to the truck.

Gage drove them away. Within minutes, he passed the entrance sign to the new subdivision, Eden Village, east of town. This was no Paradise Hills. The village showed modest raised-ranches at various stages of construction.

Gage parked in front of the office in the model home and they got out. He was very aware of Cat close beside him. He recognized the worry in the way she held herself. He longed to put an arm around her, but it wouldn't be right. He hated that something like this happened today of all days. Myer had upset Cat. It galled Gage.

Myer stepped out of the office with customers. "Well, you two look over those plans and decide which model you like best."

Gage noted the moment Myer's eyes detected Cat. For one second, the man froze. Then he switched back into charming and hustled the couple to their car and waved them off.

He turned to face Cat and Gage with an artificial smile stretched over his beefy face. "I didn't think I'd see you again so soon. Did you forget to leave something?"

Very smooth, Myer, but now I see your true colors. "This morning I wasn't aware that Hope's Garden only does business on a cash basis with Myer Contracting."

Myer tried to laugh. It fell flat.

Gage handed the man his check back. "Cash please."

Myer refused to take it and grinned at Cat. "Cat, you know I did business with your dad for—"

"Cash." Cat's sober expression didn't change.

Appealing to Cat, thinking she'd give in because she was a woman angered Gage. Gage stepped forward and shoved the folded check into Myer's breast pocket. "Cash or we load up the stock."

The man's neck turned beet red.

"Which will it be?" Holding his anger with a tight rein, Gage flexed, then tightened his fists.

"There is nothing wrong with this check!" Myer blustered.

"She called the bank." Gage folded his arms.

The change that came over Myer was almost ludicrous. The man folded up like a tent. He went back into his office.

Gage looked to Cat.

"He will be back with the cash," she murmured.

Her words were true. Myer came back. Without a word, he thrust a wad of bills in Gage's breast pocket. He marched back into his office and slammed the door behind himself.

"Count it," Cat said.

Gage did. "It's all here."

Cat looked around at the garden stock. "I don't understand him. For an extra ten percent, he could have hired us to put everything in, but he'll hire someone who does a bad job. He'll neglect to water them and lose about a fourth of the stock. I don't get it."

Gage shrugged. He had begun to make plans to put down roots in Eden. He wanted to build a solid life here. This incident had played up his weakness. It had been his parents talking when he said take the bad debt as a tax credit. But money hadn't been the issue here. Respect was. Integrity was. With Cat, issues stayed clear.

He felt he had been weighed in the balance and found wanting—though Cat would never throw it up in his face.

Cat looked glum. "Let's go. We've wasted enough time here."

He walked to the truck and opened Cat's door for her. He desperately wished he could make up for his blunder.

Inside, she snapped open her cell phone. "Hello, Chuck, how is Laurette?"

Easing behind the wheel, Gage listened intently to

one side of the brief conversation. When she hung up, he asked, "What did he say?"

"She's heavily sedated. She's not supposed to have visitors. He's going into his office for a while, then back to the hospital."

Gage nodded glumly. Would God protect Laurette and Chuck's baby? Were his prayers heard? Manny had told him so. His mood was low not only with worry for Chuck and Laurette, but it was sobering to fall short of Cat's standards of behavior. One thing he'd learned to count on was Cat's kindness. She wouldn't hold an honest mistake against him. "Cat, after we've finished planting at the Crenshaws', I'd like to show you something."

"What?"

He cleared his throat. "Some land I'm interested in for the golf course."

"Great."

He wanted to establish a respected business. But what about his larger goal? Manny had said, "Seek God first and everything else will fall into place." But how did a man do that?

Back at the nursery, the busy morning proceeded. After a lunch he didn't have an appetite for, Gage drove up the driveway to the Crenshaws' white Georgian with Cat beside him. The bright July sunlight glistened over the fashionable subdivision, a world away from Eden. In the middle of a working day, Paradise Hill was vacant, silent. No grandmothers out walking dogs or mothers weeding gardens with daughters. No grandfathers reading the newspaper on porches or mowing lawns. No children screeching as they ran through a lawn sprinkler. No toys or tools left outside. It looked like a movie set waiting for the cast and crew.

"Nice job on the showcase circle of white geraniums, Dusty Miller and roses in the front. I expected to hear 'Pomp and Circumstance' as we drove in," Cat said. Her words were light, but her dead tone revealed her continued worry over Laurette.

"Sam said she wanted formal."

"And she got formal."

He parked, and they both carried several six-inch pots of perennials and flats of flowering bedding plants to the patio in the rear. The sun heated the top of Gage's head and shoulders. Cat looked exhausted, but he knew better than to suggest she sit down on one of the wooden chairs on the patio. Cat always carried her share of the load, no matter what.

Side by side, they knelt and began planting the stock Cat had chosen, Autumn Joy sedum for green in summer and deep red in the fall, purple and white petunias and lavender alyssum for summer color, and Bleeding Heart for springtime accent. Even under the hot sun, the task normally would have had him whistling, but not today. *Call us, Chuck. Tell us what's going on at the hospital.*

"Nice." Cat sat back on her heels looking depleted from the heat and probably the anxiety, too. "Let's get them watered."

Gage nodded. Sweat trickled down his back. His leg ached from kneeling.

Taking out a blue bandanna from her pocket, Cat

wiped her face and neck with it, then resettled her dark-green cap on her sun-gilded hair.

Cat's cell phone rang. Rising, she flipped it open. "Yes?" She nodded and mouthed, "Chuck" to him. "Right. I see. Okay."

Impatiently, he struggled to his feet and waited until she shut the phone. "What did Chuck say?"

"The doctor has decided to do a minor surgery this afternoon to help prevent premature delivery."

"Will it help?" He tried to read her face for more.

"The doctor says she just has a...I forget the term, but it means her uterus just doesn't want to hold the baby very well."

Feeling a bit uncomfortable with this subject, Gage wiped the sweat from his forehead with the back of his hand. "I hope this works."

"Well, she's almost done with her second trimester. If she can make it another eight weeks, the doctor said the baby should be premature, but not too early."

His heart went out to Chuck. Gage's gut twisted. "Makes sense." He nearly touched her cheek to comfort her. Why couldn't he think of something cheerful to add?

Cat nodded, but looked near tears again. "Would you pray with me about this?"

The thought shocked him, but he managed to sound calm when he spoke, "If you think it will help."

"God said wherever two or more are gathered in his name, He'd be there."

"I don't like to pray out loud." His gut did a double twist and cinched together. Pain.

"We can pray silently. Will you hold my hand?"

He took her hand and felt that tug to hold her close. Next to him, she looked small and soft, but she drew strength from her faith. That much he'd discovered since coming to Eden.

She bowed her head and he did, also. Silently he prayed for Laurette and her baby and for his friend Chuck. Did prayer really work? Or did it just make a person feel better?

Cat whispered, "Amen." She looked up and smiled at him. "Let's get this job done."

Gage still didn't know the answers to his questions, but he knew he did feel better and that Cat looked calmer again. In his memory, he heard Manny's low voice, "Never doubt God's power." *Lord, I want to know You have power.*

Cat washed their gardening tools at the backyard hose. A spray of fine sprinkles blew into his hot face. When she was done, he took the hose from her, but didn't start watering the plants immediately. He bent over and let the icy stream of water splash over his face. Cold water coursed down his neck and under his shirt. The shock refreshed him.

"Me, too!" Cat took the hose from him and doused her face, too. She squealed. "Cold!"

How many women would do that? No thought about makeup, hairdo, just complete natural joy. Scooping her wet hair back from her face with one hand, she offered him the hose.

He took it, put his thumb over the end and sprayed a mist into her face. Instead of objecting she turned around and lifted the hair off the back of her neck, letting the spray wet her neck and back. "Ahhh," she sighed.

He couldn't take his eyes off the intimate, natural pose she'd assumed. The pale nape of her neck drew him as it had before. Would she notice if he touched—*Stop!* To break the spell, he complained, "You're no fun!"

She chuckled. "Sorry. It feels too good."

Pushing aside dangerous thoughts, he attached the plant food container to the hose and began watering. Cat wandered around the yard inspecting the shrubs and trees they'd planted. His eyes discreetly followed her. What did Cat think of him? Did she only think of him as a business partner?

From the truck, she brought one of Jo's bright copper sculptures, a row of birdhouses with one little sparrow on the end. As soon as she'd shown him Jo's ornaments, he'd seconded her decision. These ornaments promised to become an instant hit.

"Did they ask for one of those?" Gage aimed the hose away from where Cat was holding the ornament in place obviously judging its effect amid the purple and white petunias.

"Hi!"

Both Gage and Cat turned. Samantha, wearing navy cutoffs and a wrinkled white blouse, stood in the patio doorway. "I thought I heard something."

"We thought you were at work." Cat took a step forward.

"A migraine. I get about one a month. While I have it, I'm wasted, so I just stay home."

"I hope we didn't disturb you." Cat's voice showed concern.

"No, frankly the headache's nearly gone, and it's nice to see the garden finished. You two look like you've been having fun cooling off." Grinning, Sam walked out and sat down on the antique primitive garden bench. "I love it."

"Glad to hear from a satisfied customer." Gage went on watering. The first time he'd seen these two blond women together, he'd been struck by their contrast. A lot had happened since then. He saw Cat differently now somehow.

Cat walked to Sam with the copper sculpture in her hand. "I was going to put this at the end of the patio."

She reached out and touched it. "What is it?"

"A copper garden ornament handcrafted by a local artist."

"I didn't see any of these at Hope's Garden."

Gage contrasted how Cat had reacted to his hiring Hetty in April to her easy acceptance of selling Jo's ornaments. He wasn't the only one growing at Hope's Garden. Pride stirred inside him.

"We've just taken on the first consignment from the artist. The copper will turn green, you know, as it weathers and this little bird moves with the wind." Cat spun the bird.

"How clever." Sam copied the movement.

"It's our thank-you for bringing us so much business. You're a one-woman advertising campaign in Paradise Hills."

Again, Gage recalled Cat's hesitance to take on the

Crenshaws. He watched Cat's finger spin the bird once more.

Sam chuckled. "You do good work. And you stand behind it. I know sometimes I sound like a space angel, but I usually am a good judge of character."

"Well, thank you."

Gage looked over his shoulder to witness Cat's pleasure. *You deserve it, partner.*

Samantha grinned. "I was even able to eat bacon this week for the first time since you explained its origin to me."

Cat covered her smile with one hand. "Well, you asked me!"

"I know. Aren't we humans funny, the crazy ideas we get?"

Nodding, Cat pointed to the flower bed. "Samantha, we've put in annuals for color back here. After the first frost, you should come in and buy spring bulbs—"

"You mean like tulips?"

Cat spun the little copper bird on the pole again. "Yes, in fall, you pull up the annuals and plant bulbs in their place. This way next year you will have color from early March to the end of the growing season."

"Excellent." Samantha leaned back in her chair. "I'd like to have you two over for dinner sometime. You know it was a big decision pulling up roots and moving here. But more and more, Dex and I feel at home in Eden."

Gage couldn't have agreed more. Cat's grin tugged at him and his mouth curved into one, too.

"I know I always have!" Cat spun the bird, then

got up and planted the ornament firmly amidst the fluttering petunias.

An hour later, Cat dialed the nursery as Gage backed them out of the drive. The news about Laurette's surgery had eased her concern. At least the doctor was doing something. But she still felt unsettled. "Hetty, is everything okay? Good. We'll be in the field just a little bit longer." She snapped the cell phone shut and looked to Gage. "So where are you taking me? Where's this new golf course to be?" The impulse to rest her head on his shoulder tantalized her. How comforting to feel his arm come around her, to rest against this tested strength. But that was probably the furthest thing from his mind. Especially after that scene with Myer this morning. She hoped she hadn't embarrassed him.

"I have one piece of land in mind so far."

"Have you talked with the owner yet?" Buying land for a golf course meant Gage wanted to stay in Eden. The thought brought back that funny shiver that had twitched through her in April when she'd been expecting Gage. In April, she'd wanted him gone; now she felt relief that he was staying. She'd carried the responsibility of the nursery alone for two years. Having someone to share the load had turned out to be a blessing. And they had become friends, hadn't they?

Gage nodded. "The owner sounded interested. The land is zoned agricultural, so I would have to get a zoning change approved by the county."

"Have you considered you will probably have to

get DNR approval, too?'' Cat longed to trace the hard line of Gage's jaw with her finger.

"DNR?"

"Department of Natural Resources."

"Do you think the DNR would be a problem?" he asked.

"It depends on the piece of land. But I would definitely hire some firm out of Iowa City or Des Moines to do an environmental impact study." Cat decided to broach the subject that had been at the back of her mind since morning. "I hope I didn't embarrass you this morning with Myer."

"Embarrass me? No. I just felt like I let you down."

"You didn't let me down, and I know men don't like scenes." Her father had made that perfectly clear on several occasions. She studied Gage's profile. He didn't look embarrassed.

"Making sexist comments, are we, Ms. Simmons?" he teased.

"Just an observation."

"Forget about it. Myer didn't get away with anything. That's what counts."

She believed his words. She relaxed against the back of the seat.

After a few more miles, Gage slowed the truck. "Here it is, the land along the river. I thought it would make an attractive location."

Her forehead creased with misgiving, she shook her head. This land could deceive a newcomer. "No, this land floods all the way to the road here about every three years." A mental picture of the perfect acres for a golf course came up in her mind. She hesitated. It was difficult to give up a dream.

But it was an impossible dream. She'd realized that this year. In a calm voice, she said, "If you want a river view, I have a better place. Go a few more miles, then we'll take a right turn."

Chapter Nine

Gage followed Cat's directions. Iowa was approaching its peak. Green husks waving in the breeze, the fields of corn had already grown above the expected "knee-high by the fourth of July," which was less than a week away. The sun beat down on the black asphalt road creating a shimmering silver mirage always just ahead of the truck. As he drove closer to the river, the fields crested into modest green hills, some in corn or soybeans, some pasture with feeder cattle grazing. Another few country miles passed. He turned right and discovered a road he hadn't known existed. "How did I miss this? I thought I had explored every road anywhere near the river."

Cat pointed out her window. "It looks like a dead end because of the hill here."

He nodded. "Well, they always say it's not what you know, it's who you know."

Cat barely smiled. "Just follow your nose. This road will take us to the land I want you to see."

He wondered, was it just fatigue—his or Cat's?—but he felt Cat withdrawing from him. From the corner of his eye, he observed her profile. Her face held an intense but closed expression. Though her shirt still looked damp in spots, the woman beside him now appeared completely different from the lighthearted minx he'd sprayed with water just minutes ago.

Turning another bend, he left the asphalt road. He drove up a gradually rising gravel road. Another corner. He glimpsed the glittering blue river out in the distance. He stopped the car. "Wow!"

Cat nodded. "Let's get out. You will see the land and the view better on foot."

He followed her up another easy rise. Gentle hills ringed behind them. The old, lazy river curved in a wide S on the horizon. "This is perfect. Secluded, but not far off the main road."

"A river view, but no flooding to worry about."

Nodding, he couldn't take his eyes off the natural quilt of different crops—all distinctive shades of green and contrasting textures along the contours of the low hills and along the shallow valleys. *All this and the river, too.* "Who owns this land?"

"Mrs. McCanliss." Cat's curious distant attitude had intensified.

"Do you think she would sell?"

"Why would I bring you here if I didn't know it was available?" She lifted her chin, taunting him, warning him to keep it light.

Following her lead, he pulled the brim of her green Hope's Garden cap down over her nose. "Don't get smart, partner."

After the rugged night and day of worry, he allowed himself to soak in the peaceful atmosphere. The main road could neither be seen nor heard here. From here, the boom in Eden could be forgotten. Gage pictured the sculpted grounds of a good golf course. It was easy. This property was a dream come true. Someone in a canoe paddled by on the river.

Cat pointed skyward, and he watched an eagle circling on the wind. He wished he'd brought binoculars. The katydids screeched on and off. Birds chirped and one called, "to-to-to."

He brought his mind back to business. "How much do you think the owner will ask?"

Cat shrugged. "It depends on how much of this you want to buy, how much you'll actually need. You will have to talk to her."

Again that funny controlled tone crept into Cat's voice. Was he imagining it? "Where does Mrs. McCanliss live?"

Cat turned sideways. "We passed her house right after we turned. Let's see if she's home. I'll introduce you."

He couldn't read her expression. "Just like that?"

She shrugged again.

What was he missing?

"Mrs. McCanliss will be interested in meeting my partner."

He made an attempt. Perhaps this had something to do with an old disagreement. "Let me guess—you're related?"

"No, just another old family in the county. Come on."

Back in the truck, he drove them down the road. Soon he parked in front of a larger, better-kept version of Cat's white farmhouse. A big vegetable garden occupied a side yard. Tiny green tomatoes dotted green vines tied to sticks with torn rags. An abundance of red salvia and silvery Dusty Miller crowded around the settled foundation.

"Sally!" Cat called as she got out of the truck. "Sally! It's Cat Simmons." Cat knocked on the side door. No one answered. "She must be in town."

"We'll have to try another time." Disappointed, Gage tried to put his finger on it, but failed. Something was going on with Cat about this land. What?

Four days later, Gage drove Cat into town to check on Harry's progress. He parked in front of the Hadley property on maple-lined Third Street. Cat got out before he could open the door for her. They were just partners, but he wanted to do things like that for her. From comments people made about her father, he thought Cat had received little pampering in her childhood. She deserved the little courtesies she'd missed.

"It's starting to shape up, isn't it?" She motioned toward the Hadley House. The home, a Victorian castle with a tower on one end, and tall, forbidding, vacant windows, had taken on the look of an old lady in the process of a face-lift. Old scraggly trees and woody shrubs had been yanked from their stranglehold around the house giving it a naked look. Evidence of painters and roofers littered the drive to the porte cochere on the side of the house.

"Yes, just getting rid of the dead trees and shrubs

helped a lot." Gage heard his brother's whistling. Following the sound, he found Harry and Phil sitting on the unkempt grass in the shade of a spreading oak.

"Hi, bosses, you caught us sitting down on the job." Harry greeted them with the cheerful grin. "Phil and I were just taking a break. Have you heard any news about Laurette?"

"She's home again. Everything's fine. As for the slacking off, I don't blame you." Cat sat down on the grass, too. "July can be sticky in Iowa."

Unexpectedly, Ryan rode up on his bike. He looked flustered when he saw Gage and Cat. "Hi," the boy said in a guarded voice.

"Here to help us again, Ryan?" Harry asked in a welcoming tone.

Ryan, still straddling his bike, tried to look non-chalant. "Yeah, my mom said she'd kill me if I played one more video game."

Harry chuckled. "Happy to save your life, old man. Park the bike and sit down with us. I just have to report to the boss lady, then we'll get started on marking the borders and stone walk."

Ryan parked his bike against the tree and sat down next to where Gage stood.

Harry, saluting Cat like a soldier, announced, "Catherine, today we're going to get the design mapped out. With Ryan at one end of the tape measure and Phil at the other, I'll use my trusty neon orange spray paint to trace the outlines. Tomorrow we begin rototilling the flower beds."

Cat nodded. "Some of the vintage stock has already been delivered. It's at the rear of greenhouse number two."

"What do you want to plant first?" Gage asked.

Harry pointed to the southern side of the estate. "I think we'll do the herbaceous borders first."

Gage heard his brother explaining the soil preparation and planting schedule for the next month, but his real attention centered on Cat. She had risen and drifted away from them, looking at the old house. Scaffolding girded the peeling two-story house. A painter was painting the gingerbread trim around the side veranda white. Gage saw trouble. "Harry, will your gardening and their house painting collide?"

"Already taken care of, big brother. I'll follow them as they move the scaffolding around to each side. I don't want their big feet galumping through my roses."

"Good. Have fun." With a parting wave, Gage caught up with Cat. "Penny for your thoughts."

"Big spender, aren't you?" She didn't turn toward him, but continued to look up at the house.

He lightly rested a hand on a bar of the scaffolding. "Give me a sample. Maybe I will offer more."

She looked down, then bent to pull up a tall, fuzzy, white dandelion. "I was thinking about Great-grandmother Catherine. She grew up in this house." She twirled the green hollow stem between her thumb and forefinger.

He nodded, fascinated by the movement of her slender fingers.

"I wonder sometimes why she left. What happened

between her and her father to break the tie between them?''

This line of thought didn't surprise him. Cat seemed fascinated by family connections. Was that because she had lost both parents so young? "Maybe there wasn't a tie to break.''

She looked shocked. "How sad.''

He regretted his words. Though he hadn't realized it in April, she had a tender heart.

She glanced up. "I think Harry is going to do a great job.''

Grateful for the change of subject, he let a smile take over his face. In fact, he felt it to his toes. The Hadley job had energized his brother in a brand-new way.

She broached the topic he'd studiously avoided the past three days. "Hetty can handle things back at the nursery awhile longer. I called Mrs. McCanliss. She's home this morning. Want to go?''

Though her voice sounded subdued, her offer didn't startle him. He'd known she wouldn't put off taking him out there again much longer. He'd waited, letting her decide when. "Sure.''

This time Gage managed to beat Catherine to the truck and open the door for her. She rewarded him with a bemused smile.

He drove them out of the town to the flowing hills around the old farmhouse. A tiny woman, in a new blue cotton dress who looked to be an old eighty-five or a young ninety-five, waved to them from the porch. "Catherine, great to see you. Come up on the porch.''

Cat led him up the steps to the large shaded front

porch. Worn wooden Adirondack chairs and new
white plastic chairs were arranged there. Cat made the
introductions. Gage shook the thin, blue-veined hand,
then sat down beside Cat across from Mrs. Mc-
Canliss.

The old woman smiled at him, but spoke to Cat,
"What have you been doing this summer?"

"A lot of work in Paradise Hills." Cat stretched
her perfectly proportioned legs out in front of her.

"Those are some homes, aren't they?" the old
woman stated with the shake of her head. "Why
would anyone want that much house to take care of?"

"A lot of them are from California," Cat explained. "They have to roll over the profit from the
sale of their more expensive California homes into
ones here."

Gage shifted his gaze and encountered Cat's
hooded expression. A prickle of uncertainty danced
up his spine. "And the truth is, you can buy a whole
lot more house for the same money here," Gage offered.

"It certainly seems so." The woman nodded twice
and hummed to herself or had she said words? "Well,
Catherine, were you out looking at my land again?"

The way the woman asked the question and stared
searchingly at Cat made Gage think he was right.
There was something about this land that Cat wasn't
telling him.

Cat motioned toward Gage. "My partner is interested in buying it. He wants it for a golf course."

"And tennis club," Gage added.

The little woman turned keen, light-blue eyes toward him. "A golf course? You mean like when they play those golf tournaments on TV on Sunday afternoons?"

"Yes." Gage watched for the old woman's reaction.

"That's an interesting idea." She nodded twice, quick decisive nods and said something like, "Uh-uh." She looked into his eyes again. "Now, I've already had two other builders look at that piece of land for a new subdivision."

Gage's heart sank. That would raise the asking price.

"But I like this idea." She nodded twice again and made the same sound. "A golf course would be like a park, wouldn't it? A lot of people could enjoy it." She nodded again.

Gage found himself nodding along with her.

"How were you intending on financing your venture?"

This did surprise Gage. He hadn't expected business questions from this old woman.

But he replied calmly, "I have a steady income from my partnership with Catherine." Her name came out easily in this company. "I was in commercial real estate in Chicago. I'm sure I could raise enough money with investors I've done business with there for the down payment. Then I'll sell memberships with yearly dues. That would cover operating expenses and improvements."

"Sounds like a good plan." Her nodding and humming ritual came again. "I've heard good things about you." The woman eyed him sharply. "But you would have to have a membership to play golf there?''

"Since there is no public course nearby, I was thinking of having at least one public day each week. Then a nonmember would just pay a modest greens fee for that round.''

"Good. I like that.'' Nodding and humming. "That particular piece of land is so beautiful I've wanted it to give pleasure to as many people as possible.'' The old woman grinned suddenly, lifting the wrinkles of her face. "Up to now, cattle have been the only ones to enjoy that view.'' She chuckled, then turned her sharp eyes to Cat. "So Catherine, you decided you don't want to buy it, after all?''

The smell of chlorine filled Cat's nose. She drew in the scene. The church's junior high After-Nine-Night at the city outdoor pool washed over Cat—the feminine squealing and giggling, the masculine bellowing and taunting. She and Gage had come as the sponsors for their four young people. Girls chatted in clusters in and out of the water. Boys splashed the girls and cannonballed off the diving boards. "Yahoo! Watch this! I'll get you!'' *Ker-splash!* Waves of water surged over the sides of the pool, wetting Cat's bare toes on the cement apron. The gurgling, aqua-painted pool illuminated by underwater lights gave the pool area an eerie look in the darkness.

Chuck had stayed at home with Laurette who was counting the days until it would be safe to deliver. At least four more weeks were required, which equaled twenty-eight more days of lying on the boring couch.

Aunt Bet had wisely excused herself from this rowdy evening, also.

As Cat leaned her bare back against the high chain-link fence surrounding the pool, Gage lounged right beside her, only inches away. His proximity made the hair on her bare arms prickle. Inside, her emotions surged and swirled like the turbulent water in the busy pool.

Gage bent close to her ear. "I think I may go deaf by the end of this evening."

As his lips moved so near her tender flesh, her ear tingled. The suave gentleman who had landed at Hope's Garden on April Fool's Day had vanished. Cat kept her unruly thoughts to herself as she gazed at him in the deep twilight.

After a summer of outdoor physical labor, Gage— tanned and muscular—looked like a lumberjack. Or what she thought a lumberjack would look like in red swim trunks. Her lungs didn't seem to be able to expand. She took a small breath, then answered with a teasing lilt to her voice. "You'll survive."

"What?" He teased. "Did you say something?"

His warm breath fanned against her cheek. Goose bumps blossomed along her arms. She punched the nearest of his rock-hard biceps.

"Ow!"

Her intense awareness of him threatened to drown her, so she motioned toward the deep end. "Go, jump in with the guys. Ryan looks like he's about to start a fight. He has been dunking the unsuspecting."

"What am I supposed to do?"

She put her hands on her hips. "*Dunk him.* That will show him how it feels. An important lesson."

Gage shook his head. "Brilliant. Why didn't I think of that?"

She waved her hands expansively. "Some of us have it. Some of us don't."

He loped off.

Relief flooded Cat. She scanned the crowded pool area for her two charges, Morgan and Ginny. Her unwanted attraction to her business partner, her cross-currents over his buying the McCanliss property, worry over Laurette and the baby had Cat on an emotional seesaw.

To top it all off tonight, she sensed a crisis gathering with Ginny. Morgan had been subdued during the ride to the pool. Probably because Ginny had been as friendly as a porcupine. In the past two weeks, Ginny's sullenness had reached a low point. At church on Sunday mornings, Ginny's parents looked harassed. What was troubling that family?

Cat strolled around the pool trying not to look as though she were searching for her girls. Finally, she spied Morgan and Ginny with their heads together, sitting side by side on one side of a picnic table in the snack area. Their secretive pose flashed like a warning yellow light.

Cat's first inclination was to walk up and ask Ginny what was bothering her. But the direct approach with Ginny had failed every time she'd tried it. Ginny didn't want help from any adult, the enemy. Cat slowed down and sat at another picnic table behind them. *What do I do, Lord? We've had luck with the other three. I see them growing. But what about Ginny?*

Cat stared at the back of Morgan's dark hair and Ginny's lighter head. Shrill voices ricocheted around her. Normally Cat would never eavesdrop, but something about the girl's posture and Cat's desire to help Ginny kept Cat where she was. Something was warning her. Ginny needed help. But what should Cat do? *What are they saying to each other? Should I talk to her parents? What would I say? Are the girls plotting something I should hear? Lord, I just want to help.*

Standing in the cool water at the transition between the shallow and deep ends, Gage glanced across the pool. Cat wore a modest, one-piece coral-pink suit. With her abundant golden hair, tanned skin and lithe figure, she made an attractive picture. He had a hard time keeping his eyes off her.

But keeping tonight's role in mind, he picked Ryan and Phil out in the crowded pool. Ryan looked like he was wearing a flesh-colored inner tube around his pudgy waist. Phil's ribs and arm and leg bones appeared to have only skin stretched over them. Working with Harry this summer would be good for both of them.

Right now, his charges were contributing their fair share to the general din of screeches, splashes as well as the jiggling and thud of the two diving boards. His ears felt numb. But Gage continued to watch as Ryan and Phil hotdogged, taking turns jumping off the high dive.

"Hey!" Gage shouted and waved both his arms.

"Slow down! Don't get too crazy, you guys! I don't want to have to scrape you off the diving board or the bottom of the pool!"

After waving both his arms over his head in reply, Ryan held his nose and jumped in.

"His form requires a bit of work, wouldn't you say?"

Gage turned to see the senior pastor of the church in faded navy swim trunks standing beside him in the water. "Hello, sir."

The pastor, whose neck and face were dark from the sun, but whose chest and upper arms glowed white in the dim light, chuckled. "Don't 'sir' me tonight. Don't look like myself, do I?"

Gage grinned. "I wouldn't say that. From the neck up you look normal."

"The youth pastor bet me a sermon I wouldn't have the nerve to show up in my trunks."

"You showed him."

"He was going to preach for me while I was on vacation anyway, but we like to joke."

Gage followed the pastor's gaze. He was watching the future residents of the group home who were the special guests this evening. A few teens had gathered around them and were showing off their different strokes. "They seem to be enjoying themselves."

"Yes, I think they are going to be an excellent addition to Eden. We're planning an open house late in August after they've moved in. Then all we'll need to do is find them jobs. I've been talking to Mr. Burton at Venture."

Gage nodded.

The pastor folded his arms over his skinny chest. "You seem to have settled right in here, too. I hear you're interested in building a golf course on the McCanliss land."

"Cat would say Eden Gossip Central was working," Gage said lightly.

"I don't consider good news gossip. I play golf. I'll be the first in line to join your club."

"Thanks." Gage fell silent. He'd tried to find out why Cat had led him to the McCanliss land when she had evidently wanted it herself. But she had only evaded his questions. What would she want the land for? And why wouldn't she tell him?

As Gage had gone through the negotiations with Mrs. McCanliss, contacting prospective investors and commissioning the environmental study, the golf course had become more and more crucial to him. If this worked out, he'd have sunk his roots deep here. Eden would be home. Eden would be his future. But would it be at Cat's expense?

"Is there something wrong?"

Gage hesitated, then nodded. "I would appreciate your advice."

"About what?"

"When Cat showed me that land, she didn't tell me she had wanted to buy it for herself."

"I see."

Above them, Philip ran off the high dive and cannonballed, folding his knees and wrapping his arms around them. He hit the water. A mini tidal wave splashed up and over Gage and the pastor. When the waters receded, the pastor said, "You feel odd about buying the land then?"

"Yes, I don't want to take—"

The pastor interrupted, "But you're not taking it from Catherine. As I see it, she's offering it to you."

"But should I take it, just because she—"

"Catherine does have a very generous heart, but she must want you to have the land. You know the Simmons family has the reputation of being direct. Don't look for hidden messages in their behavior. You always know where you stand with a Simmons."

Gage turned this over in his mind. He couldn't argue with it. "I know. Thanks. That helps."

"Besides, you still have to win zoning approval from the county board."

This came unexpectedly. "Do you think that will be a problem?"

The pastor gave him an enigmatic look. "Perhaps you should look into who is on the board. That's my advice."

A loud piercing whistle sounded above them. "Break time!" The lifeguard shouted from his perch. "Everyone out of the pool!"

As Gage pulled himself out of the pool, he wondered about the pastor's cryptic advice about finding out who sat on the county board. Gage wanted to know. Or maybe he didn't want to know.

Through the warm August evening, Gage walked toward the local VFW Hall where the county board held its meetings. A few black, corn-fat crows squawked overhead. He felt like squawking back at them. This evening would be momentous in his life. He didn't plan to take no for an answer. But tonight he'd find out whether or not it would be a long hard journey to his goal. He'd already discovered one possible opponent. He had taken the pastor's advice and found out the names of the board members. All had been strangers—except for one name.

He had wished that one had been a stranger, too. In spite of this, he had told Chuck to stay home with Laurette. He didn't need a lawyer. Yet. The scolding crows chided him, as if to say, "So that's what you think, buddy! We've got news for you!"

"Gage!" An unexpected, but welcome voice came from behind him.

He turned to see his partner getting out of her white Hope's Garden truck. She waved. "I decided to come. I didn't want to wait by the phone."

He made a wry face at her, but his mood lifted like a helium balloon on the wind. "I know what you mean. I would like to fast-forward this evening if I could."

Wearing a sleeveless jean dress, she strolled toward him. Her skirt rippled with her movement. When had she stopped calling him Farrell and switched to Gage? He wished he could call her by her full name, Catherine. "Cat" seemed so inadequate for the warm-hearted, lovely woman he now faced.

"Worried?" She looked up at him, her toffee-brown eyes serious.

Fleetingly, he contemplated brushing the soft lips turned toward him. *Back to business!*

"Just a bit, but I've done all my homework." He

lifted a slender black leather portfolio, which he held in one hand. Offering her his other arm, he asked, "Shall we?" He almost added, "Catherine."

She took his arm. "By all means."

Gage savored the feel of her small hand in the crook of his arm. Having Catherine by his side set his confidence on high.

As they walked into the low cement-block building, he blinked to adjust his eyes to the lower light. The vinyl-floored room stretched long and narrow before them. A pop machine glowed red, white and blue in one dark corner. Folding chairs and tables on long, wheeled racks lined the dingy avocado-green walls.

The meeting took place at one end beneath long fluorescent lights, one of which flickered irritatingly. A smattering of people already sat in the metal folding chairs facing front. Five board members lounged around a narrow, folding table. Having timed his arrival with the start of the meeting, Gage now avoided looking at their faces, putting off confronting the one he knew.

As he walked toward the chairs, familiar, friendly faces turned toward him—Bet, Hetty and her husband, the pastor, Philip and his mother, and Chuck.

Gage halted. "Chuck? Who's with Laurette?"

His friend stood and slapped Gage shoulder. "Harry and Jo. They are waiting by the phone. She insisted I come."

Gratitude tightened Gage's throat. He couldn't speak, so he nodded. The support of friends meant so much. He and Cat sat in front of his supporters. Cat folded her hands in her lap and sent out vibrations of relaxed confidence. She still wouldn't discuss why she'd been interested in the McCanliss land. But that was her decision. He didn't doubt her complete support.

The county board chairman, Jim Inman, called the meeting to order. The board secretary read the minutes from last month's meeting in a dreary monotone.

Avoiding facing forward, Gage picked up a printed agenda on the seat beside him. They had scheduled his proposal dead last. He put the page back down. Then he looked into the face he'd wished hadn't been on the county board—Ed Myer of Myer Contracting.

Myer stared back at him.

When Gage had asked Chuck how Myer had gotten himself elected to the county board, Chuck had said simply, "New people didn't know his reputation." Chuck doubted Myer would win a second term. But that didn't help him tonight.

Gage smiled nonchalantly. *You don't have the power to stop me, Myer.*

Myer stared back harder and straightened his chair.

The boring meeting slogged on. A few flies and moths buzzed the lights. The flickering light made a crinkling noise. Outside, the bug-zapper crackled with action. A matter of an easement was discussed. Also a new traffic light was approved. Most of the board members acted as though they did their work completely unconscious of the sparse audience—except for Myer, who couldn't take his narrow-set black eyes off Gage.

A few people entered after the start of the meeting,

but Gage faced forward, not wanting to appear in any way anxious.

"Mr. Gage Farrell?" Jim Inman, the county board chair, finally announced. "We have your application for a zoning change. Will you come forward to answer questions?"

Gage stood up. "Yes, sir." He went forward and faced the board. He'd asked for zoning changes before. It was easy compared to figuring out Catherine's mystery about the land.

Inman smiled. "I want to say, Mr. Farrell, that your proposal is very thorough. I like that. Now you are prepared to purchase the McCanliss river property to be used as a golf and tennis club?"

"Yes, sir."

"We usually don't like to approve a zoning change for someone until the land has changed hands."

"Jim." A voice came from the rear of the hall.

Gage and the others all turned to see Mrs. McCanliss standing in the last row of chairs.

"Yes, ma'am?" Jim replied.

"Gage and I have signed papers of intent. The land is as good as his. I am not selling it to anyone else. I like the idea of that land not being developed for homes. This will be just like a park—"

"A park for the rich," Myer slipped in slyly.

"That isn't true," Mrs. McCanliss retorted. "Gage, you tell them. I've got to sit down. My knees ache, and I don't like talking at meetings." Nodding and humming, she sat down. Aunt Bet went to sit beside her.

Gage cleared his throat. "The golf course will be

open one day a week to the general public who will be able to use it for a modest greens fee. Two of those four days will be weekdays plus one Saturday and one Sunday per month. The same with the tennis court.''

"So anyone can use it?" another board member asked.

Gage nodded. "I've also talked to the high school principal and offered to allow students to be bused out to use the driving range and tennis courts in the mornings in April and May.'' That had been his partner's idea, a good one.

Most board members nodded in approval at this.

Gage continued, "To use the property, all the school would have to do to is to pay a liability insurance policy to cover the students at the course.''

The board chair held up Gage's proposal. "I see you had an environmental impact study done. Have you talked to the DNR?''

"Yes, I have their tentative okay, pending your approval.''

More nods from the row of men.

A voice came from the back again, "May I address the board please?''

"Yes, Mr. Burton,'' the board chair replied.

Everyone turned to see the president of Venture Corporation standing near Mrs. McCanliss. He must have just arrived.

Mr. Burton, dressed in a sport shirt and chinos, walked forward to address the board. "I haven't had the pleasure of talking to Mr. Farrell before now, but I have heard of his plans and I am in complete agreement. I cannot tell you how many times prospective engineers have turned down a job here because of the lack of leisure opportunities. This addition to the community will only make Eden more attractive to new residents.''

''Thank you, Mr. Burton. We appreciate your input,'' the board chair said.

Mr. Burton shook hands with Gage, then sat down.

''How are you prepared to finance this, Farrell?'' Myer snapped. ''We don't want you to get started and not be able to finish it.''

Not with bad checks, Gage wished he could say. But it wasn't possible. ''It is all there in black and white—from the down payment to the schedule of membership fees to yearly dues.''

''The plan and the figures look good to me.'' One board member looked at his watch.

''Okay, let's go ahead with the vote,'' the secretary announced.

''Wait! Wait!'' Myer objected. ''This is all just figures and promises. How do we know we can trust this stranger?''

The four other county board members looked at Myer as if to say, ''*You're* questioning *his* honesty?''

The county board chair looked around Gage. ''Cat?''

''Yes?'' She stood up.

''You're in a partnership with Gage Farrell, aren't you?''

''Yes.'' She folded her hands in front of her.

''Have you found him to be a man of his word?''

''Absolutely.'' Then she sat down.

Jim proceeded, ''Okay. That's all we need to know. Someone make a motion to vote and someone second it.''

One member declared, ''I make a motion we approve this golf and tennis club pending the successful sale of the property and final DNR approval.''

''I second.'' The secretary raised his hand.

''All in favor?'' The chair asked.

Chapter Ten

Gage held his breath.

Four "Ayes" rang out.

Gage exhaled gratefully.

"Nays?" The chair looked at Myer.

"Nay!" Myer shouted.

"Approved." The chair's expression didn't change. "All in favor of adjourning?"

Again four "ayes," one "nay."

"This meeting stands adjourned."

Gage felt Chuck thumping him on the back. Bet hugged his neck. Hetty was dancing some sort of exotic jig up and down the aisle between the folding chairs. But Catherine hung back, smiling at him. He couldn't take his eyes off her. She's stood there—golden, tanned, sweet-smiling. He wanted to break away from his well-wishers and sweep Catherine into his arms and hold her tight against him. *I love her.*

Like a rushing wind, this thought overwhelmed all

other sensations. He felt as if the floor had come up and hit him in the face. *I love her. I love Catherine.*

"I've got to get home!" Chuck declared. "Laurette is waiting."

Everything around Gage sped up. En masse, his supporters surged out of the building carrying him along like a bobber on the river's surface. He tried to reach Catherine, but she stayed on the fringe of the wave.

Desperate, he called to her, "Come to Chuck's!"

One more round. His back was pounded, he was embraced. Then everyone drifted away to their vehicles and departed. Everyone but Catherine excused themselves from coming to Chuck and Laurette's. He found himself driving away in his car.

In his rearview mirror, Gage was relieved to see Catherine following him through town instead of turning away toward her home in the country. As though nothing were out of the ordinary, Gage followed Chuck's car as they drove up their quiet street into the garage. In the near dark, Catherine parked her white truck behind them.

Gage jumped out and tried to reach Catherine's truck before she got out. He wasn't fast enough. Blast. She closed the vine-decorated door of her truck and faced him in the driveway.

He wanted to say, *I love you, Catherine!*

She tilted her head and smiled up at him.

"Come on!" Chuck shouted from the garage. "What's holding you two up?"

Cat led Gage into the kitchen. The sensation he was experiencing felt like being underwater. He could see, hear, but through an invisible buffer. He wanted to swim to Catherine and pull her in with him, then he could ignore everything else. Be only with Catherine.

"Chuck?" Laurette's voice floated from the living room. "Are we celebrating?"

"You better believe it! Eden is going to have a golf and tennis club!" Chuck hustled Gage away from Catherine and into the living room. Laurette, Harry and Jo looked up eagerly.

Gage suffered through another round of hugging and back thumping. Catherine still hung back. The desire to hold her close ached inside him. He had to regain control. A few deep breaths and his heart and lungs slowed closer to their usual rhythm.

"Time for pizza!" Harry and Jo disappeared into the kitchen.

Vaguely aware of the aroma of pizza, Gage wouldn't take a seat. He waited to see where Catherine would sit.

"Sit down!" Laurette ordered. "What's the matter with you two?"

Swallowing to moisten his dry mouth, Gage bowed to Catherine. "After you."

Catherine rewarded him with one of her dazzling smiles. She sat down on the plaid chair beside the very pregnant Laurette who reclined on the green couch.

Since he could not sit closer to Catherine, he sank into the matching plaid chair opposite her. At least he could enjoy looking at her.

Within minutes, Harry and Jo had placed a paper plate with a slice of pizza in Gage's one hand and a cold glass of cola in the other. Chuck sat on the floor by his wife with his back against the sofa. Harry and Jo sat Indian style as usual in front of the fireplace.

Gage tried not to stare at Catherine. Following everyone else, he bit into the thick slice of pizza. Warm, red sauce squirted to both sides of his mouth. He knew the pizza must be tasty, but tonight his mind couldn't take in one more sensation. Catherine, beautiful Catherine sat across from him.

"So what happened?" Harry asked. "I want every detail."

Gage shrugged and chewed slowly. If he opened his mouth to speak, he didn't know what might come out.

Catherine spoke up, "Everything went as smoothly as clockwork. Gage had everything down in black and white—"

Chuck interrupted, "Did you know that Mrs. McCanliss and Mr. Burton were coming?"

Gage shook his head and continued chewing like a dumb animal.

Catherine put her piece of pizza down on her white paper plate. "I expected Mrs. McCanliss. She likes to be in the center of things. I knew she wouldn't miss it."

"But how did Burton know?" Chuck asked the question that had occurred to Gage earlier.

"I called him and introduced myself, told him about the proposed club." Harry waved his slice in the air. "I can't believe you didn't think of that, big brother."

Still distanced from everyone, Gage wiped his

mouth with a paper napkin and took a deep breath. "Thanks, little brother."

"I don't wish to horn in on your big day, bro, but…" Harry rose to his feet in one graceful movement. "This is a day for celebrations. The Hadley estate is complete." Harry bowed with a dramatic knightly flourish.

"Ahead of schedule?" Catherine exclaimed, clapping her hands together.

This broke through Gage's abstraction. He put down his pizza, stood up and grabbed his brother's hand. He shook it vigorously. "That's great!"

Harry's face split with a broad smile. "I am really pumped! I feel like I have conquered the world."

"I know what you mean." Gage tugged his brother into a quick back-slapping hug. He felt himself coming back to the shore, bit by bit.

"Save some of that. More congratulations are in order." Harry pulled away from his brother, then offered his hand to Jo. She took it, and he drew her gracefully to her feet. "Jo and I are engaged."

Gage's mouth dropped open. "But you've only known each other for two months."

Harry tucked Jo close to his side. "It only took two days."

Jo blushed prettily and hid her face in Harry's shoulder.

Gage stared. Too much was happening. Too much…

Her eyes wide-open, Laurette propped herself up on her elbow. "When is the wedding?"

Harry kissed his fiancée's forehead. "Jo finishes

her masters degree next May. We'll be married in June.''

"You're staying in Eden, too?" Gage gasped.

Nodding, Harry explained, "Jo's father is the president of Eden College. We had a long talk when I asked him for permission to marry his daughter. I plan to commute to Iowa City to complete my doctorate in fine arts. In the meantime, I've been asked to continue as groundskeeper for the Hadley estate. Fanny is going to start up her bed-and-breakfast soon, so I'll have to move out. But Bet has agreed to rent me a room so my living costs will be minimal. That's the plan.''

Gage couldn't take it all in. His brother had always been a drifter, not really grounded in reality. Love had changed him.

Gage didn't feel the same, either. He gazed at Catherine. What would she say if he told her, "I love you"? He'd been blindsided. What if Catherine wasn't interested in expanding their partnership to a personal level? He couldn't ask her to marry him out of the blue! What if she looked at him like he was an idiot? If that happened, how could he face her every day at Hope's Garden? How could Harry be so confident about love while his big brother floundered?

Laurette began to cry.

"What's wrong?" Chuck leaped to his feet.

"Nothing. I'm just happy. Everything is fine." Laurette smiled and wiped her eyes with her yellow paper napkin. "Oh!" she exclaimed suddenly. "I have a great idea!"

"What?" Gage watched Laurette.

"A garden party! You and Cat can combine the celebration over the groundbreaking for your golf and tennis club and the completion of the Hadley House garden restoration!"

Chuck clapped his hand on Gage's shoulder. "That's a great idea, honey! Gage, you can invite those investors out from Chicago to see what they've invested in and attract a huge crowd, not just from Eden, but from the surrounding county. You'll be inundated with people wanting to buy memberships!"

Laurette took over. "And it will be great advertising for Hope's Garden! Cat and Harry can show off what they've done! We'll invite people from the state historical society! It will knock everyone's socks off!"

Harry cleared his throat. "I have something more to add to this occasion." He waited until everyone looked toward him. "My intended—" he paused to kiss Jo's ear, making her blush again "—has created a large copper sculpture to grace the Hadley garden. This would be the perfect occasion to unveil it."

"A sculpture!" Laurette squealed. "How wonderful!"

More congratulations were exchanged.

Gage and Catherine were the only two serious people in the room. Gage tried to analyze what his partner was thinking. Personally, he was thinking of hugging Catherine. He tried to move. His feet had taken root.

"Well, don't just stand there!" Laurette scolded. "What do you two say?"

"I could never organize something like this right

now, Laurette," Cat spoke up. "This is my busy season. I've got tons of jobs in Paradise Hills—"

"You wouldn't need to do anything, but show up. I'll organize everything from right here on the couch."

"Honey, I don't want you overdoing it," Chuck cautioned.

"I'll just be dialing the phone and giving orders. In fact, this may keep me from going insane in the next month."

Jo volunteered, "I'll help and I'm sure my mother will, too. She's always entertaining, the wife of the prez, you know." She grinned.

"And I'll help, too," Harry offered. "I'll just be doing odd jobs till school starts anyway."

"So?" Laurette demanded, staring at Catherine.

Catherine looked to Gage. He shrugged.

She conceded, "Okay. When?"

"We need to get permission to use the Hadley grounds. We need to give people at least two weeks' notice," Gage suggested.

"Okay!" Laurette agreed. "I'll just need a guest list from you—"

"Wait!" Cat stopped Laurette. "We need to set a budget first." She looked to Gage. "I'm willing to use your partnership payment this month for this—"

"But—" Gage objected. "I wanted that money to cover the expenses on the Hadley job."

"No argument. Your brother brought it in just under budget. We'll manage." With a playful frown, Cat shook her finger at him.

"Okay, but I'll match it," Gage insisted.

"Great!" Laurette took over again and declared as though announcing the winner of a contest, "The Eden Golf and Tennis Club's Groundbreaking will take place three weekends from now with a garden reception afterward at the Hadley estate!"

Cat gazed at the happy faces in the room. All the news this evening had been good, the best. It was selfish, but with Gage starting another business she felt as though she'd be losing him. She'd become accustomed to working with Gage. Now he'd spend less time at Hope's Garden, and in a few years, she'd pay him off and she'd be on her own again. She wondered how this would affect Hope's Garden and her...heart.

Finally, Chuck and Laurette's house was quiet and dark again. The pizza had been eaten and the guests had left for home. Gage sat in his basement room on his narrow twin bed.

Still feeling a bit at sea, Gage lifted the cordless phone and dialed his parents' number. His mother answered.

"Hi, Mother, it's Gage."

"What's the matter?"

"Nothing." He couldn't very well tell her, *I've just realized I'm in love with my business partner.*

"Are you certain?"

Yes. "I just wanted to tell you my good news." *What do I do now? How do I find out if Catherine feels anything for me?*

"Good news?" his mother sounded wary.

"Yes, I've gone ahead with that golf course idea I

discussed with Dad." He hurried on to prevent her from dashing cold water on his plans. "I want to invite you and Dad to the groundbreaking and reception in three weeks from this weekend."

"In three weeks? So soon?"

"Yes, I'm inviting my investors from Chicago and I'd like for you and Dad to come out, too." Everything he said was factual but it still felt like a dream—except for Catherine. Loving her was real.

"Well, if it's that important, your father and I will come out, of course. You know, we've only wanted you to be successful and happy. If a golf course in Iowa will do that, of course, we'll come."

"And I think you'll be pleased when you see what Harry has accomplished here, too." Right now Harry's life made more sense than his did.

"Harry?" His mother's voice sharpened. "I'm happy to hear he is still alive. He hasn't called or sent us so much as a postcard."

"He's been really busy, but I won't tell you doing what. I think we'll save that as a surprise for you when you arrive."

"All right and maybe I'll have a surprise for you when I come."

Gage chuckled. He pictured his mother meeting Jo, her future daughter-in-law—the buzz cut, five earrings and all. *Mother, Harry has a real surprise for you.*

"Would you reserve that bed-and-breakfast for us again—both rooms? I don't want to share a bath with a stranger."

"Sure. I'll send you an invitation, Mother. Give my best to Dad."

He hung up and looked around the shadowy basement, the lonely, empty space. He hadn't been able to hold Catherine close tonight or tell her he loved her. He didn't know when he would be able to. Soon? Never? He didn't have a clue. But he had called his mother and shared the good news about the club. That would please Catherine. He laid back on his bed and stared at the exposed beams overhead. Why hadn't he seen falling in love with Catherine coming? One thing he knew for sure. Daria had never had this effect on him.

Three weeks later, as Cat stood sorting the day's cash income into piles of ones, fives, tens and twenties on her desk, her mind went over the events of the coming weekend—the open house at the group home, the groundbreaking at Gage's golf course, and the reception at the Hadley House garden with the unveiling of Jo's copper sculpture. This week Laurette had called incessantly with last-minute details. Even standing here alone, Cat felt jumpy, on edge.

Her phone rang. Wondering what Laurette wanted now, she lifted the cell phone from her pocket. "Hope's Garden. We have every bloomin' thing you need. Cat speaking."

"Catherine, we have some bad news—"

Cat recognized the senior pastor's voice and froze. Laurette!

The senior pastor went on, "Ginny Claussen in your youth group has run away."

The relief that it wasn't an emergency concerning Laurette made Cat's knees rubbery. She sat down at her desk. Just as quickly, concern for Ginny flooded her. "When?"

"She was supposed to visit a friend today, so her mother didn't miss her until late this afternoon. When her mother called the friend's house to tell Ginny to come home early, the friend's mother said she hadn't been there at all. Everyone has been called. No one has seen Ginny today."

Cat murmured, "I've been worried. I could tell she wasn't happy." Cat recalled Ginny's sullen face. The girl had never shown even one real smile to Cat.

"I was wondering if you have any idea where she might have gone."

Cat combed her memory. "I'm sorry. She hasn't confided in me."

"If you think of anything, please call me at Ginny's home. I will be staying there tonight until Ginny is found. They think she may have gone to her father in the Quad Cities, but they haven't been able to reach him. He's away on business. Please pray. Her mother and stepfather are frantic."

"I will. I'm so very sorry." Cat snapped the phone shut. She bent her face into her hands and prayed, "Dear Lord, please protect Ginny. You know where she is. Keep her safe from harm and help her to be found soon. Comfort her family." Cat imagined what Ginny's parents were suffering. Losing a loved one— Cat knew that sinking, irrevocable feeling too well. She wrapped her arms around herself, chilled in spite of the humid high eighties temperature.

"What's wrong?"

Gage's voice made Cat look up. "Ginny ran away."

"No." He hurried over and pulled Cat up and into his arms.

She huddled close to him, drawing comfort from the soft cotton of his shirt against her cheek and his solid reassuring strength. She murmured, "I feel so guilty. I sensed something was going to happen. I saw the signs, but I didn't know how to step in or if I should."

"I know. I felt the same way."

His deep voice rumbled through her since her ear was pressed against his hard chest. She pulled back and looked up into his face. "We have to do something."

"But what?"

Reluctantly, she stepped out of his embrace. "We need to talk to Morgan. I think Ginny told her about this at the night pool party. I overheard bits and pieces of their conversation. I didn't want to eavesdrop, but I was worried."

"Let's go." As he dragged her toward the nursery's door, she managed to snag her purse and tell Hetty to close that night. He opened the passenger door to the truck. She climbed in and he drove off.

Longing to move closer to him, Cat twisted the strap on her leather purse. "Anything could happen to her." Images of faces of abducted children on posters loomed in her mind. She sealed her mind against the dreadful realities of what could happen to lost or unprotected children.

"Don't worry. We'll find her."

Gage's firm statement reminded her that she could count on her partner in a crisis. He was that kind of man.

Within minutes, Gage pulled into the drive in front of Morgan's small white house flanked by tired pine trees. He hoped Catherine was right and Morgan could help. They hurried to the house and knocked. Morgan opened the faded red door. The minute she saw their faces, fear and guilt filled her eyes.

"You know where she is," Cat stated.

"No—"

"Morgan, you can't lie for her. This is too serious." Cat took Morgan's shoulders in both hands. "I don't think she went to her father's apartment in Illinois. Where did she go?"

"I told her I wouldn't tell..." Morgan sounded close to tears.

Gage spoke up, "You don't have a choice. You know even going as far as the Mississippi River is too far for a thirteen-year-old alone. Now tell us what you know."

Morgan began to cry, tears slid down her round cheeks. "I told her not to do it."

"Do what?" Gage insisted.

"She said she hated all her parents, and she was going to leave. But I didn't think she would really do it."

"Morgan, did she say how she was going to get away? Was she going to hitchhike?" Cat probed.

The young girl rubbed her reddening eyes. "She

said there were truck stops on I-80 where you could pick up rides and go all the way to California.''

Cat bent her forehead to touch Morgan's. "Oh, no."

The two syllables sounded as though drawn from deep within Catherine. Longing to comfort her, Gage instead rested his hand on the teen's trembling shoulder. "Any other lead you can give us?''

"She mentioned Mount Pleasant, too. A truck stop there. I didn't think she'd really go through with it.''

Gage said, "Okay, we're going to call Ginny's family and tell them what you've told us, so they can give this information to the police.''

Morgan looked frightened. "I won't get into trouble? I've been worrying ever since the church called to tell us to pray Ginny would come home or be found. Mom started telling me about what can happen to girls when they run away. Then I was…too afraid to tell…Mom that Ginny had talked to me. I mean…I don't know where she is…." The girl broke into tears.

"Don't worry," he reassured her. "Your mom will forgive you, but we need to give this information to Ginny's family.''

Morgan's mother arrived home from running errands, just as Morgan was finishing her recital of what she knew to the sheriff over the phone. Leaving the weeping girl with her mother was a relief. Morgan was safe. But where was Ginny?

Gage and Cat, still keyed up, walked outside into burnished twilight. A neighbor mowed his lawn. The tranquillity of the evening magnified the engine noise.

A dog barked. A bicycle bell *chinged*. On this peaceful street in the small Iowa town, fear for a child seemed out of place, alien.

"Cat, should we pray about this...I mean..."

She took his hand. "Let's."

"I still don't like praying out loud." He gave her a half smile.

"We'll both pray silently. Only God needs to hear us."

He nodded. Her hand in his gave him a feeling of connectedness he needed now. After a few moments of meditation, he opened his eyes to find her toffee-brown eyes gazing into his. "How far is Mount Pleasant from here?"

"About an hour's drive."

"Do you think Ginny would have had any luck hitchhiking there?"

Cat considered this. "I think she would have been afraid to hitch close to town because people would have asked her questions."

Running away in a small town would be difficult. "So you think she might have walked for quite a while first?"

"Yes, to get out where she wouldn't be recognized."

"And walking would slow her down." Hope flickered inside him. Finding a girl on foot sounded more reasonable. Cat nodded, watching him.

He forced a smile for her. "The state police can cover I-80 better than we can. I think we'll drive down all the roads on the way to Mount Pleasant in our Hope's Garden truck."

She looked puzzled. "Why? I'm sure the police are doing that—"

"Yes, but Ginny might be having second thoughts, and she might react like Morgan just did now—"

"How do you mean?"

"They are still kids. Morgan's first thought was 'Will I get into trouble?' That's probably what Ginny's thinking about now."

"Okay. Go on."

"So if Ginny sees our white truck with Hope's Garden on the side, she'll recognize it immediately. And she might flag us down. We aren't as frightening as a police car and she knows we would help her. Right now I think she'd be in the mood to listen to us."

Cat threw her arms around him. "You're brilliant! It just might work!"

He relished her embrace. Her fine golden hair, fragrant with herbs and blossoms, tickled his nose. He brushed her hair with his lips, but so lightly she wouldn't notice. The past few weeks had been agony. When would he get enough courage to tell her he loved her? He eased back. "I don't know about you, but I can't just sit around wondering. We may not find Ginny, but at least this will give us something active to do."

"Let's go."

That's my Catherine! He opened the door for her and she got back in the truck. He resisted the urge to place his hands around her waist and give her a boost. *Patience. Now isn't the time. But soon, very soon.* As he drove them to the road out of town to the south toward Mount Pleasant, Cat dialed Ginny's number and told the pastor their plan. She hung up. "He said he wishes us well. And Godspeed."

Gage nodded. Twilight began to mute the late August sun's brilliance. Cat got out her Iowa map and folded it to show them just the southeast quadrant where they hoped to find Ginny. After Gage had driven out of town into the almost unbroken fields of head-high corn, Cat pointed to a possible side road Ginny might have taken to another Iowa two-lane highway.

Sitting on one leg with her back against the door, Cat held the map and pointed directions at intersections. Gage drove on. The tall corn, green and golden with ripe silk, loomed up on each side of the road like walls. When Gage halted at each red stop sign, the din of the grasshoppers closed in around them. The screeching cicadas added their noise to the busy summer evening sounds.

After an intense hour of driving up and down different county roads, Gage pulled into a lone gas station at a crossroads and bought them a fresh supply of soft drinks. Cat filled the green-topped cooler on the floor, then the search began again.

Another silent, tense hour. Gage pulled to the side of the empty asphalt road and helped himself to a fresh can of cold soda from the cooler. He rolled up his window and turned on the air-conditioning against the heat and insects. "I feel like I'm getting lost."

Cat looked at him in the gathering dusk. Her hair glowed in the low light. "I'm wondering if Ginny might have, too."

Gage considered this. "That's right. She doesn't drive yet—"

"So she probably doesn't pay attention much when the family drives out of town," Cat continued.

"That means we should probably drive down every road in the south of the county."

"Yes, even dirt or gravel roads that aren't dead ends."

The thought of the young girl walking down road after lonely road, afraid to stop and ask directions tugged at Gage's sympathy. In daylight, the cornfields held no mystery. But at night, any breeze through the husks could sound ominous, eerie. A young girl's imagination could conjure up all sorts of dangers lurking in their cover. The kid might be hysterical by nightfall.

Or she might have already gotten to Mount Pleasant or I-80, hitched a ride with a trucker... Gage didn't want to go down that road. He was sure ninety percent of American truckers were decent men and women, but there was no guarantee that Ginny wouldn't find one of the questionable ten percent. Bad things happened every day. Nasty headlines from the past flashed in his mind.

They would find Ginny. He drew in a deep breath. "Which way?"

Cat directed him to the right at the fork ahead. He drove down yet another dusty gravel road. The air-conditioned-cool hush inside the truck weighed on him. Glancing at Cat, he read the way her shoulders drooped. Worry must be eating at her tender heart.

A thought occurred to him that would distract them

both. "Cat?" When would he have the courage to call her Catherine?

She glanced at him.

He hoped he wasn't making a mistake. "May I ask you a question?

Chapter Eleven

"What?" Cat turned her eyes on him.

He took the last swallow of sweet soda and discarded the can in the plastic trash bag hanging from the dash. "What did you want the McCanliss property for?"

She sighed and stretched her supple legs out in front of her. "I was wondering when you'd get around to asking me that."

"You didn't act like you wanted to tell me," he said, aggrieved because his careful discretion looked like it hadn't been needed.

"I know." She stopped.

"Are you going to tell me now?" he prompted.

"It's no big deal. I've just loved that property since I used to go on hikes with my friends."

"What did you want to do with it?" he probed. Her pat answers didn't fool him. Why was she hesitating?

She stared out the window, her profile pensive. "Do you remember once you asked me if I wanted a ranch with horses and cowboys?"

"You don't mean that!" He couldn't stop this from flying out of his mouth.

"Well, not the cowboys." She grinned at him, the waning sunlight nearly abandoning them. "But I've always wanted a ranch-style house on a rise above the river and a stable with a few horses."

"Horses?" he mused. The road took an unexpected curve. They rattled across an old wooden bridge over a creek invisible in the growing shadows of darkness.

She nodded, then sat up straighter. "Slow down. Something moved in that pasture." She motioned toward the right.

Gage slowed. "I don't see anything." He stopped the truck anyway.

Cat jumped out and called, "Ginny? It's Cat. Ginny?"

No answer. The corn husks on the other side of the road rustled in the night breeze.

"Ginny?" No answer. Reluctantly, Cat climbed back into the truck cab and shrugged. "I guess it was just some animal, a raccoon or something."

He started up again. The road dipped and followed its wide curve.

Gage picked up the topic again, "Your ranch-style house and horses seems like an achievable goal. I mean, you won't have the McCanliss property, but otherwise what's the problem?"

She gave a deep sigh. "Time, money, the usual things that hold people back."

"I didn't even know you rode."

"I don't. Not really." She stared out her window. "I wanted to have a horse and lessons when I was eleven. But my dad said a horse was too much money and wasted too much time. Horses take a lot of care and eat a lot of feed."

Gage felt a catch in his throat. Cat had loved her father and loved him still, but Gage thought her life would have been easier if her mother had lived to soften her father. His family had worked the opposite way. His father at crucial times had stepped in to check his mother. Was that why God gave a child a mother and a father—for that balance?

"You aren't feeling guilty, are you? That's why I didn't tell you." She sounded worried.

"I suppose a little."

"Don't be." She waved his concern away with her hand. "I couldn't afford the land now and by the time I could, Mrs. McCanliss would be dead and the land sold to a builder for a subdivision. I realized that before you even came to town. It was just a dream."

So he was building a golf course on Catherine's dream. She deserved her dream, but by now the land was bought and zoned! Catherine's generous heart revealed itself again. "I don't know what to say, but thank you. That land is perfect."

"Don't mention it. Besides I agree with Mrs. McCanliss. I like the idea of a lot people being able to use and it enjoy that view." Cat continued staring out the window on her side, obviously alert for any sign of Ginny. "And I'm glad you're staying in Eden."

Her words flowed through him like sweet honey. She'd finally said the words he'd wanted to hear. She wanted him to stay in Eden.

Dark had fallen on southeastern Iowa—corn and soybean fields, old faded barns, lonely farmhouses spotlighted by a single, high pole lamp, and one-street towns shut down tight for the day. They stopped for gas. On her cell phone, Cat called Ginny's home number. The teen still hadn't been found. State police were circulating a faxed photo to be posted at all the truck stops on I-80.

Starting off again, Cat wondered if she and Gage would run out of back roads before they found Ginny or heard she was home safe and sound. Cat didn't want to contemplate any other possibility.

After she'd admitted to Gage why she'd wanted the McCanliss land and that she'd wanted him to stay in Eden, they had driven on in a friendly silence. Both of them vigilant, scanning both sides of the road, they only exchanged words when they came to a cross-roads where she told him which direction to go.

The cab of the truck had become a separate little world, set apart from the solitary country roads and the problem that had brought them out here. That must have been the reason Gage had asked her about the McCanliss land. There had been a freedom in letting him know that she valued him and wanted him to stay in Eden, but there was also a hidden fear. What if he didn't care whether or not *she* cared? Tonight would he, too, lift the curtain which concealed his past?

She decided to chance it. "Gage?"

"Yes?"

She said a quick prayer. "Who was Manny?"

"I told you, didn't I? He was my first boss." Gage's voice sounded nonchalant.

But she knew him too well by now. "There's more to it, isn't there?"

He let his breath out in a rush. "That is an understatement."

A flicker of victory flashed through her. He trusted her. "Would you tell me about him?"

Gage nodded slowly. "His name was Manuel Ortiz. He'd come from El Salvador to America with his parents when he was just a child. By the time I met him, he was a grandfather. He owned his own lawn maintenance service and did my parents' lawn and gardening for as long as I could remember. Before I even started kindergarten, I would watch for his truck each week and run out to follow him around. He liked kids and always had a candy bar for me."

Cat grinned in the glimmer of the moon's early light. "I'd have followed him around, too."

Gage chuckled and leaned back. "Anyway, when I was about eleven, he started letting me tag along with him in the summer to help with other lawns and gardens. My mother was ill that year, and I didn't have much supervision. I think that's why Manny let me go along. Kept me out of mischief."

"You speak as though Manny has passed on."

Gage's hand went to the cross on the chain around his neck. "Yeah, three years ago. But the bond we forged that summer stuck. I worked for him every summer after that—much to my mother's distaste. Right through the summer after I graduated from college.''

"I wish I had known him.'' She almost added, "He was the father of your heart, wasn't he?''

"He would have loved Hope's Garden.''

"Did Harry work for him?'' The mystery of Harry's expertise with gardening needed explaining, too.

"Yes, though I think he did it just to irritate my mother, but that's how he learned gardening.''

"Manny was more than your boss, wasn't he?'' *Open up. Tell me, Gage. Please.*

"Why do you say that?''

"I hear your respect and love for him in your voice.''

Gage cleared his throat. "Manny was one of a kind. He taught by example. From the time I was little, he talked to me like I was a real person, like I mattered. He took time to show me what he was doing and tell me why. He lived life as an honest and well-loved man. At his funeral the church was packed, literally standing room only.

"He had a deep faith. I can remember being around eight years old when he showed me how to plant my first tulip bulb in the fall. He told me about how Christ had been buried, then later had risen. He gave me the picture from the bag of bulbs to save till spring when the tulips would rise and bloom. That memory is so vivid, I can still feel the soft, moist dirt under my small fingers. He always said to me, 'Seek God first and everything else will fall into place.'" Love resonated in Gage's voice.

Cat blinked back tears. "Good advice."

Stretching his arms out straight, Gage pressed his hands flat against the steering wheel. "But how do you do that? I've been trying to figure that out. How do I put God first in my life? I mean, I know I'm not the type to go to seminary or something like that. I love to do the work Manny taught me."

"Putting God first—anyone can do that."

He hit the steering wheel with his palms. "Well, tell me how! I mean it! How does running a golf course mesh with God?"

Cat sat up again. "What's that?"

Gage stepped on the brake pedal.

Cat jumped out. A stray-looking white dog barked at her and retreated into the cornfield. She got back into the truck. "Sorry. I just saw movement in the brush again."

"Don't apologize. We don't want to take the chance of missing Ginny tonight." He drove on.

Cat mused over Gage's words just before they had paused. How did a golf course and God go together? Folding both legs under her, she drew closer to him. "You asked how to put God first in your life." She watched for his reaction to let her know if he wanted her to go on.

He nodded.

"Gage, it's a matter of how you do things, not what you do. You're an honest man, Gage. That's one way to put God first. Another is the way you've offered to share the golf course with the young people of

Eden. Asking yourself what would please God, asking Him how to love your neighbor as yourself. I don't know how to say it any different.''

As Gage smiled, his teeth gleamed white in the moonlight. ''That's not a bad attempt. You make sense.''

''Stop!'' she shouted. Would this be just another false alarm?

In the darkness beside the country road, stepping out from a stand of trees along a cornfield, a young girl waved her hands frantically.

He slammed on the brakes again.

''It's Ginny. Thank God!'' Cat touched Gage's shoulder as she breathed a deep sigh of relief.

''Thank God is right.''

Throwing open her door, Cat jumped out and rushed to the girl. Sobbing wildly, Ginny staggered into Cat's open arms. Gage caught up and pulled both of them into a tight embrace.

The humid heat of the summer night enfolded them. For seconds, all Cat could do was cling to Ginny. Gage's strong arms encircled them like a strong shield. Cat's prayer of thanksgiving poured through her heart beyond words. The prodigal had been found. The weeping could end and the rejoicing would begin as soon as they got her home.

Cat took a deep steadying breath. ''It's all right, Ginny. We found you. We'll take you home.''

Still, Ginny clung to them. Huddled around her, Cat and Gage waited. Finally Ginny's wrenching sobs turned into hiccups. ''I'm so tired and thirsty.'' The girl swayed.

Gage caught her and swung her up into his arms.

Cat tugged the dusty black backpack off her shoulders. "We'll give you something to drink and get you home right away."

He carried Ginny to the truck and gently set her in the middle of the seat. Cat scrambled in the passenger door as Gage climbed in and slammed his door, the sound loud in the night.

Ginny lay crumpled against the seat. "I saw your truck.... I couldn't believe it was you." More hiccups and stray sobs. "I've been walking and walking.... I got turned around—"

Snapping open the cooler's green lid, Cat handed Ginny a cold root beer. "Drink this. You'll feel better."

With shaking fingers, Ginny popped the tab and drew in a long swallow. "My stepdad is going to kill me!" Tears ran down her dusty cheeks.

Cat tugged Ginny close and wiped her face with a paper towel. "No, you'll probably get grounded, but everyone—including your stepdad—is worried sick."

Gage did a U-turn on the empty country road and headed north. Ginny tried to smile at Cat, then drank the soda.

With Ginny settled warm against her, Cat pulled out her cell phone and dialed Ginny's number to give the good news to the pastor. Ginny's mother cried so hard that she couldn't speak.

The stepfather took the phone from her. "Thank you. Thank you," he repeated, then he broke down.

Ginny managed to stutter a few words, then she couldn't stop crying.

Folding up the phone, Cat calmed her down once again. Soon Ginny rested her head on Cat's shoulder and fell asleep from the exhaustion and worry of a day of being lost and lonely.

"Poor kid," Gage murmured.

Cat nodded, then stroked the mussed blond hair back from Ginny's face. "I have a feeling that Ginny's family is going to be ready to talk to the pastor about family counseling."

"What a difference a day makes."

Cat went still inside remembering losing her father on a night like this. She shook off the memory. Why was she thinking about that now?

"That's how I felt after my boating accident last summer."

Cat froze. She'd never asked him about the accident, which had evidently changed his life. It had seemed too private. "I know you lost a dear friend."

"Yes, Gary. He was one of our foursome at the university. Losing him—it didn't feel real for a long time."

Her heart overflowed with sympathy. If anything happened to Laurette, she didn't know how she could bear it. "You weren't able to attend the funeral," she said softly. "You were laid up for months Chuck said."

Gage nodded, his chin hard by the dashboard light. "Maybe if I'd been able to attend the funeral, it would have been real to me. I still keep thinking that I'll give Gary a call. Then I remember he's beyond my reach."

Oh, Gage. She longed to hold him close, comfort him. "You didn't blame yourself, did you?"

"I still do—"

"But—"

"I know, it's irrational." His voice was sharp. "I wasn't at fault. We were wearing life jackets. The other boater was drunk, and he plowed right into us. I couldn't have done anything different." A pregnant pause. "The jerk only got scratched."

Intuitively, she sensed this wasn't private anger, but righteous indignation against the injustice of this sometimes cruel world. "But he's in jail, isn't he?"

"Yes, when you kill someone, there is a price to pay."

Cat thought everyone involved had paid a high price, but that was understood. She could do nothing but offer sympathy. "I'm sorry."

A gust of a sigh came from deep within him. "Don't be. I guess good can come out of anything. It shook me out of the rut I'd fallen into when I got out of college. For that and *only that*, I'm grateful."

Just after midnight, Gage drove up to Ginny's brightly lit house. He noted that several other homes still had lights on also. In a small-town neighborhood, no one slept easy while a neighbor paced the floor for a runaway child. He lifted the sleeping girl from the seat and carried her to the house. The cool air revived her. She woke up, blinking in the light. He put her down just as her parents rushed out the front door to pull her into a three-way hug.

"Oh, Mom, I'm so sorry!" Ginny wailed.

Gage hung back. Cat came up beside him to watch the reunion. Before they could be noticed, Gage tugged her away. She followed his lead and they slipped away before being drawn into the scene.

As he drove away, he glimpsed neighbors at their windows, joyful witnesses, too.

"Thanks. I didn't feel like a prolonged round of thank-yous." Cat sounded exhausted.

Feeling the same dragged-out sensation, he nodded and yawned.

She tapped his shoulder. "Don't drive me all the way home. I'll just sleep on Laurette's couch tonight. It's too late for you to drive all that way out and back."

"But—"

"No argument."

With Catherine, he knew this wasn't just politeness, she always said what she meant. He grinned. The night had been rich with emotion and a growing intimacy. He'd told Catherine what lay closest to his heart. He wondered why he'd held back so long. Her calm words had been a blessing, the sharing, a deep relief. "Okay, boss lady."

Within minutes, he drove into the familiar garage next to Chuck's car. In the dark narrow garage, he tugged Cat out of the truck through his side. She slid down to stand beside him.

He turned to her and said, "There's something else."

She looked up. "Oh?"

He leaned down and kissed her.

Cat couldn't catch her breath. She closed her eyes, concentrating on Gage's kiss. His lips moved against hers like dragonfly wings. She couldn't move. If she did, she might break the exquisite contact. Everything within her held its breath, too. Did her heart still beat? Yes, she felt a pulse in her finger tips.

Or was it his heartbeat under her hands? His shirt lay under her palms. She splayed her fingers wide and pressed them down on his rock-hard chest.

His lips pulled away.

"No," she objected.

He buried his head in the crook of her neck and brushed his lips on her tender nape. "Catherine, my sweet Catherine."

She took a little gasp of breath. She shivered. Her hands slid up to the column of his neck. "Gage."

Lifting his head, he pulled her into a full embrace. He kissed her lips again. This time his kiss grew persuasive.

The light blazed on. "Is that you, Gage?" Chuck's voice boomed in the silence. "Did they find Ginny?"

Cat squeaked and jerked backward, bumping into the truck.

Gage tugged her back close to himself again. "Chuck...we'll be in, in a minute."

"We'll?"

Cat's heart pounded. What would Chuck think?

"Catherine is with me."

"Catherine?"

"Cat, my partner. She wants to sleep on your couch. It's been a long night. We found Ginny and took her home." Gage shielded her from Chuck.

"Great!"

"Chuck, go get a pillow and blanket for Catherine."

"Anything wrong?" Chuck sounded puzzled.

Cat blushed red-hot.

"No, you interrupted us. We'll be in in a minute."

"Okay." Still sounding confused, Chuck shut the door to the kitchen.

Gage smiled down at her. "Chuck always had lousy timing."

Cat couldn't meet Gage's eyes. What was Chuck telling Laurette right now?

"It been a long night." Gage brushed his calloused thumb over her bottom lip, igniting sparks in her. "So I won't keep you out here. But there are two things I must say." He gazed into her eyes.

A warm, a sweet glow coiled through her. "What?" she whispered.

"Number one, you're very special to me, Catherine. Very special." With his index finger, he lifted her chin. His touch danced through her making her chin quiver.

"Number two?" Now she couldn't take her gaze from his face. His scrutiny of her stirred up more vague sensations and longings.

"We will take this up again very soon."

The passionate look in his eyes made her knees go weak.

He slowly released her, but he threaded his fingers through hers and led her into the house. It was the first time Cat had ever wished to avoid her cousin and Chuck.

Gage's kiss had blown apart her world. She wanted to ask him a thousand questions. But right now, she couldn't speak of it. It was too new, tender, precious.

An hour later, Gage lay on his narrow bed in the basement. The house was quiet at last. Laurette and Chuck's questions about Ginny had all been answered. They'd been too polite to comment on Gage's holding Catherine's hand all the while they talked. But their eyes had communicated their approval.

He gazed at the unfinished beams overhead. In the room above him, Cat lay curled up on Chuck's green couch. So near and yet so far.

Well, I kissed her. I called her Catherine. She didn't slap my face or tell me to knock it off. That much he had accomplished. *Where do I go from here, Lord? How do I make her my partner for life?*

The next evening Cat sat at her desk staring vacantly at the day's cash. All day she'd felt as if a fast-moving freight train had barreled into her life. It had snagged her, then like clothing on a line tied to the end of the caboose she flew along behind.

All day, work and other obligations had kept her and Gage apart. They'd waved and smiled at each other in passing once or twice.

Last night, Gage and she had brought Ginny home. *Gage called me Catherine.*

Today was the open house at the group home.

Tomorrow the groundbreaking at the future golf course and the garden party took place.

Last night she'd had maybe two hours of sleep. *And Gage kissed me.*

Today everyone in Eden had called or dropped in to congratulate her and Gage and thank them for helping bring Ginny home. Or at least, it felt like everyone.

Gage said I was special, very special to him.

She stared at the money in front of her. *I should count this.*

Hetty drifted in, her purple gauze skirt fluttering around her. She looked at the clock over the door. "There's only a half hour left of the open house." The young, very pregnant woman shook her finger at Cat. "I am closing tonight."

"I'll never make it. I don't have time to go home and change—"

"Just go wash your hands and face and brush that head of thick hair of yours," Hetty ordered.

Cat was too tired to argue. She rose and went to the small bathroom off the office. Cold water on her face refreshed her a little. As she brushed her tangled hair, she examined her face critically in the small mirror. A summer in the sun had left her hair blond-streaked and her face brown and freckled. Obviously Gage had chosen to kiss her in the dark for very obvious reasons.

She squirted her juniper body lotion on her hands, spread it over her neck and face, too. She finished by fingering on tinted-pink lip gloss. "Don't overdo it, Cat," she murmured, then sighed. What could Gage see in her? She wasn't beautiful. She wasn't smart.

Discouraged, she bid Hetty good-night and drove

into town. Seeing Gage was what she wanted most right now, but a tautness filled her. It was like the feeling of tension in a movie when she feared the heroine might make the wrong choice. And if she saw Gage, he might kiss her again. That was both wonderful and terrifying. Everything would change forever.

Parking her truck down the crowded block, Cat tried to hide her anxiety as she strolled toward the group home. Lights gleamed in the windows of the freshly painted, newly occupied white raised-ranch. Two pots of lemon-yellow marigolds flanked the bottom of the front steps. Harry and Phil had also groomed the lawn, old shrubs and trees. Laughter and the chatter of voices spilled out the open windows and front door.

As she stepped inside, Kevin, one of the residents, greeted her. "I remember you," he said, "you were the one with the boy and girl painting each other yellow."

Cat chuckled and greeted him. She scanned the crowded living room for Gage. She heard his voice, but couldn't see him.

Another resident, the plump young woman, drew her toward the buffet table loaded with finger food and red punch in a huge bowl. She insisted Cat fill a plate with canapés, deviled eggs with paprika sprinkled on them, crisp carrots and celery sticks and a piece of chocolate cake.

The young woman looked at Cat's shirt and read the name out loud, "Cat. Is your name really Cat?"

"No," Gage's voice came from behind. "Her name is Catherine." His arm claimed Cat's waist.

She nearly spilled her punch. "Hi," she gasped.

"I've missed you," he murmured next to her ear.

Gage's touch zipped through Cat's whole being. Instantly, the fatigue and confusion that had weighed her down all day evaporated. Every cell of her body seemed to expand. She'd never felt so alive before.

"I can't wait to take you home," Gage whispered. "We have some unfinished business we need to discuss."

Cat quivered inside. The kiss last night hadn't been just her imagination. Gage no longer saw her only as a business partner and friend. A happy, warm glow radiated from her.

Morgan's mother bore down on them. "You two are wonderful. Thank God, you went out looking for Ginny."

"We couldn't have just stayed home and waited. We were too keyed up," Cat explained. She looked down at her plate full of food. Gage's touch had filled her up and she couldn't take a bite.

As though reading Cat's mind, Gage lifted a ham salad canapé and held it to her lips. "Eat this. I bet you've been too busy all day to eat."

What could she do? She accepted the crisp, salty morsel. Gage's fingers touched her lips, a tantalizing torment.

Morgan's mother observed their exchange, then drifted away, wearing a knowing smile.

"Hey!" Ryan approached. "Those are real good. My mom made them."

Gage kept Cat within the circle of his arm, but he reached over and took one off Ryan's plate and popped it into his mouth. "Delicious. My compliments to your mother."

"Hey! You've got your arm around Cat," Ryan pointed out loudly.

Cat cringed inside. Couldn't Ryan talk a bit quieter? Did he think he was the town crier or something?

Gage chuckled. "I told you this kid was smart."

Ryan studied the two of them. "Does that mean you guys are going to start dating or something like that?"

Cat felt herself turn pink. Around her, friends glanced discreetly at them, smiled and turned away politely.

"Something like that." Gage stole another canapé from Ryan's plate and popped it into Cat's mouth.

Cat was dead certain that everyone in the room had picked up on that remark. People were still talking, but more quietly as though not wanting to miss any of Gage's outrageous words.

"My mom and dad are coming with me tomorrow to the groundbreaking out at your golf course and then the garden party. Mom's bringing her camera to shoot pictures of what I did there." This last information was said rather diffidently. Was Ryan uncertain as to the "coolness" of his mother photographing him in public?

"That's wonderful," Cat spoke up. "Harry bragged about you and Phil. He couldn't have finished so efficiently without you two."

Ryan's chest lifted with honest pride. "Thanks. I really got into it. Harry knows all that gardening stuff."

"Maybe you can work at Hope's Garden part-time next summer," Cat offered, trying to focus their conversation on a different topic.

Ryan hesitated. "Well...I was thinking of trying to get a job as a caddie at the golf course. Phil said caddies get tips."

"An excellent idea." Gage punched the boy playfully on the arm. "Read up on golf over the winter. Watch some tournaments on TV. In the future, I plan to hold a caddie training session. But it will be two years before I open for the first season."

"Okay. I'll be ready by then!" Ryan's face looked completely happy for the first time. "I'll go tell Phil. Hey, Phil!" The teen rushed off.

Gage tugged her a bit closer. "I can't wait to get you to myself. Why don't you eat that food, so we can get out of here?" He fed her a bite of creamy-looking deviled egg.

Cat felt everyone in the room gazing at her. Did Gage realize he was publicly staking his claim on her? This wasn't something to do lightly in a town Eden's size.

"It's true!" Morgan came over and stared at them. "Ryan said you were hugging Cat."

Cat nearly choked on deviled egg.

"This isn't hugging," Gage informed Morgan airily. "I'm saving that for later."

Morgan looked startled, then grinned. "Cool. Way cool. Wait till I tell Ginny. She'll freak."

"Gage," Cat warned him in a hushed undertone.

He leaned closer. "Did you lead me on last night? As I remember, you kissed me back. So don't toy with me now."

"Hey!" Morgan interrupted. "Harry's girlfriend made a statue for the Hadley garden. Is it really a naked lady?"

Gage laughed out loud.

"Morgan," Cat scolded, "where did you get such an idea?"

"That's what Ryan told me." Morgan gave them a disgruntled look.

"Ryan doesn't know anymore than the rest of us," Cat said. "The copper sculpture will be put into place tomorrow morning and unveiled at the garden reception in the afternoon." *Jo wouldn't do a nude for the Hadley garden, would she? This was conservative Eden, not Iowa City!*

"Security will be very tight," Gage teased. "No one but Harry and Jo have seen it."

"Okay." Morgan nodded.

Just then, the senior pastor came up and tapped Gage's shoulder. "Hate to interrupt you two, but I need one more word with you about tomorrow."

Gage nodded, then whispered in Cat's ear, "Finish that food. When I'm done, I'm taking you home." He kissed her ear, then strode away.

He's done it now. Cat sighed. No one could mistake that gesture!

"Wow," Morgan breathed.

Cat echoed this silently. She picked up the rest of

the deviled egg from her plate. Gage wouldn't take her home until she ate.

"Gage, darling!" A strange woman's voice carried over the buzz of the crowded room.

Cat looked at the front door. A tall, brunette in a white linen suit sailed into the room and made a bee-line for Gage.

"Gage, it's so good to see you again!" The brunette threw her arms around Gage.

Cat froze. She recognized Gage's parents and brother entering the door. The whole room fell silent.

A huge diamond rock...ring flashed on the brunette's ring finger.

Gage said, "Daria?"

Cat dropped her deviled egg.

Chapter Twelve

The next afternoon at 3:00 p.m., the groundbreaking ceremony was about to begin. Gage stood on the portable platform looking out over the crowd that had come to witness the beginning of his new venture, his dream. As a fitting background for the celebration, Iowa was at its zenith. Tawny sunlight shone down on ripe green fields. Brown, white-faced Herefords grazed on hilly pastures overlooking the river. Drops of sunlight glinted and danced on the blue river. The scratchy clamor of grasshoppers filled the air.

Uncomfortably warm in the August humidity, Gage in his best business suit searched the crowd for the one person whom he wanted to be here most of all—Catherine. She hadn't shown up yet. Had something come up so she hadn't been able to close Hope's Garden early? He couldn't imagine her not coming. Not even after Daria's performance last night.

He'd called her at home twice last night. No answer. Then arguing in heated whispers with his parents in their room at the bed-and-breakfast had kept him busy until too late to drive out to Catherine's house—especially since she might not be there. She had dozens of friends and relatives she might have spent the night with.

Besides, what he had to say to Catherine, he wanted to say in person when they both weren't half-asleep. And with Daria on her way out of town. But why hadn't Catherine answered her phone? Did she somehow think he'd invited Daria. No, it wasn't possible.

He glanced at the front row of flimsy metal-and-plastic folding chairs. His parents sat there. At their side perched Daria, decked out in a striking red suit. Outrage still smoldered inside him. He blamed his mother more than Daria. His mother's meddling had hurt Catherine last night. That would not happen again.

But today, he'd been busy every minute greeting and entertaining his out-of-town investors. He had worked for and with all these people in Chicago. They'd all invested in this venture on his word alone. He couldn't slight them now. But it had left him no time to call Catherine to arrange to meet for a real conversation.

What's more he didn't have the opportunity to remind Daria that *she* had ended their engagement months before and to ask her to take his ring off. He hadn't ever expected to see Daria wearing his ring again. He'd realized he should never have proposed to Daria in the first place. He had felt a little guilty over that. He didn't feel guilty today, and today that ring would be off Daria's finger once and for all!

Gage combed the crowd once more, but Catherine's sun-streaked head was not present. A glance at his watch and Gage approached the microphone on the platform. "Good afternoon, friends. I'm so happy you all have come to share my joy. In a moment, several people who have been instrumental in this project will symbolically break ground for Eden's first golf and tennis club.

"It is difficult for me to believe that I have only lived in Eden since April of this year. The challenge of making a place for myself here has been exciting and thought-provoking. Eden is a unique commingling of people—the longtime residents, those associated with Eden College and the new professionals. I believe it will prove to be a successful blend for its future. Now to the groundbreaking."

After applause and introductions, Gage, the mayor, Mr. Burton of Venture and the president of Eden college stepped down from the platform. The photographers for the county paper and for the *Eastern Iowa Gazette* followed them and flashed pictures.

Harry, also in a suit, one he'd borrowed from Gage, waited beside the platform on the highest knoll of the river property with a brand-new shovel in his hand. First the mayor, then the software entrepreneur, then the college professor took turns digging up a token of soil. As they finished, Gage shook their hands one by one. More applause. More photos.

Gage took the microphone again. "Thank you all for coming today. Now I'll turn over the microphone

to Pastor Conkling of Eden Community Church."
They shook hands again and Gage sat down.

The pastor faced his audience. "Don't worry,
everyone, I didn't prepare a sermon." Laughter.

Gage glimpsed a white Hope's Garden truck
parked in the distance. Quickly he scanned the gathering. There she was! Catherine, still in her work
clothes, stood to one side. Instantly, Gage's frustration with the situation his mother and Daria had created evaporated. He could always count on Catherine's good sense and loyalty. Catherine didn't sulk!
Then he thanked God she arrived in time for the pastor's announcement. He knew she would be thrilled
with it.

The pastor continued, "It has been my pleasure to
get to know Gage Farrell this summer. He immediately became involved in our church's summer small-
group youth program. You all know that two weeks
ago he and Catherine Simmons searched for Ginny
Claussen on their own and brought her home.

"That night, even though he could have left the
matter to others, Gage took action to help his neighbors. That epitomizes the kind of man Gage Farrell
is. He and I have had many conversations recently on
how to seek the kingdom of God first in his life. Putting God first in your life is embodied in the two
greatest commandments—to love the Lord with all
your heart, soul and mind and to love your neighbor
as yourself.

"Gage has demonstrated this already in his service
to Eden by planning ways for the whole community
to benefit from the golf and tennis club. Today I'd

like to thank him also for hiring three of the residents of the new group home to work as part of his grounds crew here." Applause drowned out the rest of the pastor's words. Another round of handshaking took place.

Finally Gage took the microphone again, "Now, everyone, please join us at the garden reception at the Hadley House. The garden restoration is complete and the unveiling of the garden statue will take place promptly at six this evening." More applause.

People milled on both sides of Cat. Shading her eyes from the sun with the printed program, she watched her partner shaking hands with the mayor of Eden. She couldn't take her eyes off Gage still speaking to the three groundbreakers. In a crisp white shirt and dark suit, Gage seemed like another person. Not at all like the man she had spread manure with. Not the man who had sprayed her face with water on the Crenshaws' patio. Not the man who helped her find Ginny. Today he looked like a man who could be engaged to Daria.

Gage looked around. Was he looking for her? Catherine knew the instant Gage picked her out of the crowd. Beaming, he started toward her, but was stopped by well-wishers. He waved to Cat and sent her a special smile. Feeling a warm blush go through her all the way down to her toes, she waved back. This was Gage's day of triumph. Cat tried to get through the crowd to him, but people also stopped her to congratulate her on the garden restoration.

In the distance, Gage's parents and Daria claimed

Gage and drew him with them to the gold-toned luxury sedan. Still smiling at Cat, he motioned toward town. She nodded and waved back. Then he got in the car. It drove away.

"Who are those people anyway?" Mrs. McCanliss stood at Cat's elbow.

"Those are Gage's parents," Cat replied. Her brief elation slipped a fraction as the sedan slid from sight.

"Who's the woman with all the makeup?" Mrs. McCanliss stared after the car.

Thinking of the gossip potential Daria presented, Cat said diplomatically, "That's a friend of the family."

"It's clear she wants to *be* family." Mrs. McCanliss nodded her head and hummed in a gloomy tone.

Cat didn't know what to say to this. Daria's behavior did lack a certain subtlety.

"She won't fit in here in Eden. That's for sure."

Cat agreed, but again, what could she say? She shrugged.

"If I'd known she was part of the deal, I wouldn't have sold him the land. Doesn't he have enough sense to marry you?" Mrs. McCanliss demanded.

Cat stared at the old woman. How could she answer that $64,000 question?

"You two make a good pair." Complaining further to herself, Mrs. McCanliss hobbled away.

The old woman's words stuck in Cat's mind. She and Gage did make a good pair. Mulling everything over, she drove home, showered and changed into her new sleeveless, yellow cotton-broadcloth dress. After

Daria's dramatic entrance last night, Cat had driven to the new strip mall to buy a new dress. With the picture of Daria's chic suit vivid in her mind, Cat had needed a sizable boost to her self-confidence.

The bodice of the simple tie-back dress Cat had bought was embroidered with a colorful garden and had seemed perfect for today's garden party. Now alone in her bedroom, Cat gazed at her reflection in the full-length mirror. While Daria had looked bold and sophisticated, Cat looked small-town and quaint.

In her mind, Cat played back last night's scene. Daria had rushed in and thrown herself into Gage's arms. The look Gage had sent Cat had been one of complete shock and dismay. Instantly, that had been replaced by acute embarrassment. Obviously, he had realized how Daria's arrival would look to everyone after the message his behavior toward Cat all evening had been announcing to the community. Then Daria pops in! Poor Gage had immediately hustled Daria and his parents out of the group home. What else could he do?

Cat had heard her phone ring twice late in the night. She'd guessed it was Gage calling, but she hadn't wanted to talk to him over the phone. What they had to say to each other was too important for a phone call. Hesitating while her phone rang, she'd realized she'd wanted to discuss Daria face-to-face.

Still pondering, she drove downtown. Cars already lined the streets near Hadley House. Wanting to see Gage immediately if not sooner, Cat tamped down her frustration, parked and walked the four blocks. In addition to the new dress, the saleswoman the night before had talked her into buying a rolled-brim straw hat with a matching yellow ribbon around the crown and a new pair of stylish sandals.

As Cat trudged toward the party, the new sandals rubbed a nasty blister on her heel. *That's what I get for trying to compete with Daria.* Cat reached the wrought iron fence around the Hadley grounds. Glancing up at the tall, vacant windows, she thought of her great-grandmother. *What would you do, Catherine, if a man told you, you were very special, kissed you, then his fiancée popped up wearing a diamond the size of a rutabaga?*

No answer came.

The dead could answer no questions. But Cat didn't need one. Daria wouldn't have daunted great-grandmother. And Cat believed Gage. He hadn't said he loved her in so many words, but today as he had searched the crowd for her, his eyes had said it plainly.

He loves me, doesn't he, Lord? He wouldn't have invited Daria without telling me. His mother obviously has been meddling again. I can see Daria would be her perfect choice for a daughter-in-law. And Cat could see how a man might be tempted by an old flame....

No. Cat shook her head. Gage was not the man he'd been in April. He couldn't be the same man now who had once proposed to Daria. *I'll just have to face Gage, Daria and his parents and believe Gage loves me. I'll take another step of faith.*

Gage's love was a gift from God and Cat wouldn't

doubt it. God loved her and so did Gage whether she wore fancy shoes or not!

Cat walked through the front gate, slipped off her painful sandals and dropped them neatly in the midst of a group of new shrubs. Daria didn't belong in Eden. With or without shoes, Cat belonged here and Gage thought her special. Cat strolled in, feeling incredibly free as her bare feet padded over the sun-warmed, stone garden path and cool grass. She chuckled to herself. *Gage's mother thinks I'm a hick anyway. Why disappoint her?*

All around Cat, her design and Harry's hard work shouted, "Job well done!" The renewed garden flaunted tender new saplings and shrubs, lush green leaves of all textures, shapes and sizes, dozens of varieties of blossoms in a rainbow of reds, pinks, purples, whites, yellows and golds. With Bet's help, Harry had added antique garden seats and a birdbath, also bird feeders of all kinds. Over the hum of human voices, birds swooped and chirped and chattered. Three squealing children played tag on the front lawn. Great-grandmother would have been pleased. The scene brought a smile to Cat's heart.

Most of Eden and the county had shown up. Cat looked around but couldn't find Gage.

Aunt Bet greeted her. "Did you feel like going au naturel today?"

Cat paused and, lifting her midcalf skirt a couple of inches, pointed one toe as if posing for a shoe ad. "You must be referring to my lack of footwear."

Bet moved closer and motioned toward the rear of

the garden. "Yes, but the question of the day is who is that *lady in red* hanging all over Gage?"

Cat followed Bet's motion and saw Daria clinging to Gage's arm as he talked to the local state congressman. Gage moved away from Daria. The former fiancée looked irritated and pursued him. *She's certainly persistent.*

Cat looked away. It had nothing to do with her. "That, Aunt Bet, is Gage's former fiancée."

"Former?" Hetty joined them with her happy silent husband in tow. "Then why is she wearing—"

"I know," Cat interjected. "The rock."

"Exactly." Bet opened her eyes wide.

Cat shrugged. "It really has nothing to do with me."

Hetty stared at her.

"I'm thirsty. I need some punch." The late August sun had passed its peak, but the summer heat and humidity still held its sway. Cat walked to the buffet table set up in the shade. She accepted a cup of green punch and sipped its cold sweet lemon-lime.

Bet followed her. "Laurette was going to try to come in a wheelchair, but she just didn't feel up to it."

"I'm so sorry." Cat's happiness dimmed momentarily, but Laurette's long wait was nearly over. The doctor had said the baby could come safely anytime now though the due date was still a month away. "She did such a wonderful job and you, too, Aunt Bet. Everything is just great!"

Hetty came up. "I can't help it. I need to know!

What do you mean that woman has nothing to do with you, and why are you barefoot?''

Cat grinned. ''I'm barefoot because I have a blister, and Gage is well able to take care of his former fiancée.''

''Sounds logical to me,'' Hetty's husband spoke up for the first time. ''You're a smart woman not to make a fuss. Gage looks hunted by that woman. I feel sorry for him.''

Hunted! Cat giggled behind her hand. Bet chuckled and Hetty hugged her husband. Cat waved farewell and took her refilled cup of green punch and wandered over to the side veranda and sat down on the middle step. Out of the corner of her eye, she saw Gage and Daria in deep discussion under an arbor near the rear of the lawn. Neither of them looked happy.

Cat turned her attention to the rose garden. Harry had planted already budding bushes early in the project so mature roses in deep maroon, light pink, white and yellow bloomed sweetly fragrant.

''Hi, Cat.''

Cat looked up at Ginny. Cat leaped up and hugged the girl close in welcome. ''How are you?''

''Better.''

Cat settled back down, and Ginny sat beside her. Cat was relieved Ginny's mother wasn't with the girl. The mother's effusive expressions of gratitude had embarrassed Cat. After all, God had just used Gage and her to answer all the prayers for Ginny's safe return.

Cat scanned Ginny now and pronounced, "You look very pretty today."

Ginny smiled. "Mom took me shopping, and we bought this." The girl fingered the skirt of the simple pink dress she wore. "You look pretty, too."

Leaning back on her elbows, Cat stretched out languidly on the steps. "Thank you."

"I like your hat."

To make Ginny smile, Cat hopped up and put one hand on the crown of her rolled brim straw hat. She struck a mock model pose. "Très chic, don't you think?"

Ginny giggled.

The lovely sound opened Cat's heart wide. She offered the girl her hand. "You are, too. Come on." Ginny took her hand and Cat drew her up to stand beside her. Together, they posed as though modeling for a fashion shoot.

More giggles bubbled out from Ginny—fresh and free. Cat joined her.

"Catherine!"

Cat glanced over the railing.

The senior pastor waved at her. Beside him walked a photographer and a reporter. "Here she is. Catherine, they want to do a story about you for the *Gazette*."

"Me?" Cat straightened up. "Why?"

"I told them you were a direct descendant of the Hadleys. In fact, you're named after your great-grandmother Catherine Hadley."

"And your nursery did the garden restoration for

the grounds?'' The man with his pencil raised over a notepad asked.

"Yes, Hope's Garden did the design. But Harry…Harrison Farrell, Gage Farrell's brother, did the research and actual work."

"Gage is your partner, isn't he?" The man jotted as he spoke.

"Yes, he is."

The photographer poised his camera to his eye. "Smile."

Though Cat normally would have been too shy, today she felt on top of the world or at least, on top of Eden, so she smiled.

"Walk down the steps," the photographer, hidden behind his fancy camera, instructed.

Cat sashayed downward, inwardly chuckling.

"You're barefoot?" the reporter pointed out.

"Yes," Cat said in mock seriousness. "That's to symbolize my great-grandfather, the poor dirt farmer, whom Catherine Hadley married."

The reporter chuckled. "The farmer and the banker's daughter. Sounds like an interesting match."

Leaning on the railing, Cat regaled the reporter with the story of Catherine proposing to Joshua Simmons and even Catherine's experience as a mail-order bride and the dirty undershirt that had sent her back to Iowa. People gathered to listen. The reporter scribbled furiously while the photographer took shot after shot.

Out of the corner of her eye, Cat glimpsed Gage at the edge of the crowd, grinning at her. The formidable fiancée in fire-engine red was nowhere in sight.

"Gage, darling!" Cat called out imitating Daria's performance from the previous evening. She felt like adding, "It's so good to see you again!"—the rest of Daria's words. But Daria had embarrassed him enough last night and perhaps Gage might not see the humor in it so soon.

Grinning, Gage started for her. The crowd parted to let him through.

Cat turned to a reporter. "This is my mail-order partner. I thought about wearing a dirty undershirt to scare him off, but it's turned out just as well that I didn't."

Gage stepped up beside her. His eyes gleamed with amusement. "I wouldn't have been daunted that easily." He leaned close and whispered in her ear, "I think you should take your shoes off more often."

"Flattery will get you nowhere, sir. I'm not that kind of girl." Cat took on the pose of outraged innocence. She whispered back, "Where is your fiancée?"

"I don't have a fiancée—yet," he replied only to her. He turned to the friendly faces gathered around them. "It's time for the unveiling. Let's move over there. My brother, Harry, will be announcing it shortly."

Gage drew Cat along with him. His arm around her reassured her that her heart had been right. In the center of the garden, a white-sheet-covered sculpture waited. What would it be?

Harry and Jo, along with her beaming parents, stood beside it. Jo wore a gauzy yellow dress for the occasion and reminded Cat of a bright-eyed daisy.

"This is the finale of a very special day," Harry spoke loud enough to be heard. "I am a newcomer to Eden and feel honored to have been a part of the restoration of these grounds to something approaching their former beauty. Jo Handleman, the daughter of Dr. Handleman, the president of Eden College, has donated her artistic talent to embellish this garden in Eden." Harry tugged the sheet away.

An appreciative "Ohhh!" sighed through the people encircling the sculpture.

The same sound filtered through Cat's parted lips. "It's beautiful!"

The two-dimensional copper sculpture depicted a Victorian lady in a long ruffled dress who held a parasol. The lady glanced over her shoulder as though flirting with an unseen gentleman.

Spontaneous applause broke out. Cat heard Ryan and Phil wolf-whistling madly, even though it wasn't a naked lady. Tucked close to Harry, Jo looked especially pretty as she blushed.

"They make a great couple, don't they?" Gage tugged Cat closer, settling his arm more securely around her waist.

She glanced up at him askance. "What will your fiancée say if she sees you hugging me in public?"

"I told you, Catherine, I *don't have* a fiancée. I haven't had one for more than six months." He tightened his grip on her. She made a face at him.

Harry waved. "Gage! Catherine!"

Gage pulled her forward along with him. "Yes, brother?"

Harry had drawn Nikki and Duke over to Jo and

her parents. Nikki looked suspicious of Harry's motive.

"Isn't this a lovely party, Nikki?" Cat asked in her best society hostess voice.

Chuckling, Harry winked at Cat. "Mom, Dad, Jo has done me the honor of accepting my proposal of marriage. We plan to be wed next June."

Nikki looked like someone had hit her in the face with a wet fish.

Duke recovered first. "Wonderful! That's great!" Beaming, he shook Harry's hand, then kissed Jo's blushing cheek.

Nikki glanced at Jo's parents, then smiled. "Yes, it is." She kissed Jo's cheek, then turned to the Handlemans. "It looks like we're going to be related."

Cat made the inference. Now Nikki could go home and tell her friends, "Gage has started his own golf course and Harry is marrying the daughter of the president of Eden College." Even after Nikki's meddling, Cat was happy for her. Maybe a wedding and the possibility of a grandchildren would help Nikki learn to relax and enjoy her family.

The cell phone in Cat's pocket rang. She pulled it out. "Hello?"

"Cat?" Chuck's voice sounded breathless. "We're at the hospital. Laurette's water broke. She's in labor. This is it!"

"I'll be right there." Cat snapped it shut.

"What is it?" Gage asked.

"Laurette's in labor at the hospital."

Evidently, Gage had the identical reaction she did.

"Let's go! My truck's in the alley." As he pulled her along, he shouted what was happening to Harry.

The round clock on the wall of the waiting room read twelve past 1:00 a.m. She and Gage were finally alone, sitting again on the uncomfortable tan plastic chairs in the quiet hospital. Upstairs, Laurette and Chuck labored together birthing their first child. Hetty and her husband and Aunt Bet had gone home to their beds at last. Cat rubbed her eyes.

"Now we can talk," Gage grumbled.

Cat yawned. "All right. Start explaining about Daria and the rock."

Gage slid his arm around her shoulders. "What has got into you, Catherine? You've been in a funny mood—"

She punched his arm. "Stop stalling."

"Ow."

"Fess up. Now."

He shrugged. "My best guess is my mother made Eden sound attractive, *very attractive* to Daria."

"Eden?" Cat tucked her chilled barefeet under her. "Attractive to Daria?"

"I believe Mom portrayed Daria as becoming a big fish in a small pond, the new Eden country club set. Also here, since the cost of living is still lower, Daria could have the mansion she's always wanted and the shopping in Minneapolis or Chicago is less than an hour's flight away."

Cat stretched then leaned back against Gage. Being near him brought her contentment. She wasn't even worried about Laurette in labor. All would go well.

Her healthy baby would be born today. "I don't get it. What has that got to do with you?"

Gage's face lit up. "Exactly! Daria evidently thought all she had to do was show up with the ring on her finger and I'd forget about the breakup."

"I would have thought she'd have known you better." Cat considered him and stroked the hard line of his jaw feeling the growth of his beard. She contemplated all that had happened in the past twenty-four hours. One thing stood out. "Gage, I was so pleased about your hiring some of the young people from the group home."

"Catherine Simmons, you do know me well, and I knew it would make you happy."

"That's your way of seeking God first?"

"One way. I finally understand what the pastor said today. Putting God first isn't always in the big things. It's in all the little choices that add up to the good of your neighbors. I finally feel I'm where I'm supposed to be, doing what I've always wanted to do. My only regret is that Manny can't be here to enjoy it. He would have loved Hope's Garden and you, too."

Gage leaned over as though to kiss her, then paused. "I love you. Will you be my bride?"

"What would you do if I said no?" She leaned her nose forward until it touched his.

"I wouldn't believe you." He kissed her sunburned nose.

"You told Daria you loved her, too, didn't you?" She waited for his reaction.

Gage's face sobered. "Catherine, I didn't know

what real love was then. I got all mixed up for a while, but the accident—''

She pressed her fingers to his velvet lips. "I understand."

He took her hands in his as though they were tender young seedlings. "Catherine, don't you know in this plastic world, you're twenty-four carat gold?" He kissed the calluses on one palm and then the other.

Cat felt tears sting her eyes. Gage had dared her to grow, to try new ways. She thought of the Crenshaws, the gardening software, the Hadley House bid. This summer she'd taken more than a few steps of faith.

Now her day had come, too, because of Gage's challenging her. Gage was heaven-sent. "I love you, Gage Farrell. And I'll be your bride."

Chapter Thirteen

The next afternoon at the window of the baby nursery on the second floor of the hospital, Gage settled his hand possessively on the back of Catherine's neck. "She's so tiny."

Reveling in his affectionate touch, Catherine gazed through the glass at Laurette and Chuck's daughter. "She is five pounds three ounces."

"My point exactly."

"What do you expect? She was a month early! But she's big enough to go home tomorrow." Catherine smiled and scratched the glass with her finger. "Hi, sweetheart. Hi, little Cassie."

Gage brushed his lips over Catherine's ear.

"Don't do that," Catherine whispered. "You'll embarrass us."

"Impossible." Taking her chin in hand, he turned her face to his and kissed her.

She pulled away. "Someone might see us."

"Who cares? I can't believe you are the same woman who yesterday went to the garden party barefoot."

"I was in a funny mood yesterday." Catherine lowered her eyes and blushed.

"Yes, and everyone in Iowa is reading about it today. So don't get shy on me now." The photos of barefoot Catherine had appeared on the front page of the *Gazette*'s "Iowa in Person" section that morning.

Catherine leaned her cheek against his broad chest. "I'm so happy, Gage. I didn't know I could be this happy."

"I'll be happy December first. That's as long as I'm waiting for you." He kissed her hair. Then turning her so her back was to him again, he wrapped his arms around her waist.

Safe and warm, Catherine murmured, "It's long enough. We'll have the reception at Hadley House. They'll have the first floor renovated by then."

Gage grinned. "Yes, I think great-grandmother would like her namesake to celebrate her wedding there."

"And it will make your mother happy."

"More importantly, we will be together. A family." He bent and kissed her hair.

"A family," Catherine repeated. A shiver of joy rippled through her. "I'll have a family again."

Peeking at her from the side, Gage cocked an eyebrow at her. "We can start working on that as soon as December first if you like."

Catherine's gaze drifted to the baby behind the

glass. In an awed voice, she said, "Oh, my, we could have a baby next year."

"If you want to," Gage added.

Catherine nodded. "We'll talk about it."

Gage kissed her. He cleared his throat. "The one thing I regret is that since I'm just starting up a new business, money will be tight for a few years. I won't be able to build you that ranch-style house and stable by the river yet. But you're going to get your dream. I saved a piece of the McCanliss property for us to build on."

"Gage, a house is just a house. As long as you and I are together, we'll make a home. My house will welcome a fifth generation."

"It will also welcome a new roof, gutters and a fresh coat of white paint." Gage grinned and tapped her nose.

"Well, well, this is interesting." The senior pastor stood beaming at them. "Young man," he said with mock sternness, "are your intentions honorable?"

"Positively." Gage pulled Catherine under his arm and kissed her cheek. "I found my perfect mate in Eden."

Catherine suppressed a giggle. "We're making it a partnership for life."

* * * * *

Dear Reader,

Thanks so much for picking up *Hope's Garden*. It is my third Love Inspired title, but my first book set in my home state, Iowa. I hope I have given you a flavor of life in the Heartland, the rolling hills, blue rivers and green fields of corn.

The themes of putting God first in your life and loving your neighbor as yourself are intertwined. Cat took Gage on as a partner because of business concerns, but she didn't realize that God had brought him into her life for more than business. Both Cat and Gage needed to learn how to put their lives in the right order—considering God first and their neighbors before themselves. Not an easy lesson to swallow.

I know I struggle with these lessons in my own life. What helps me is always trying to remember that what I do to others, I am actually doing to God. Scary thought, don't you think? How wonderful that when we fail, God loves us enough to pick us up, brush us off, forgive us and give us another chance. I've often heard that our God is the God of the Second Chance. For that, we can all be truly grateful.

Please write me at: P.O. Box 273 Hiawatha, Iowa 52233

Lyn Cote

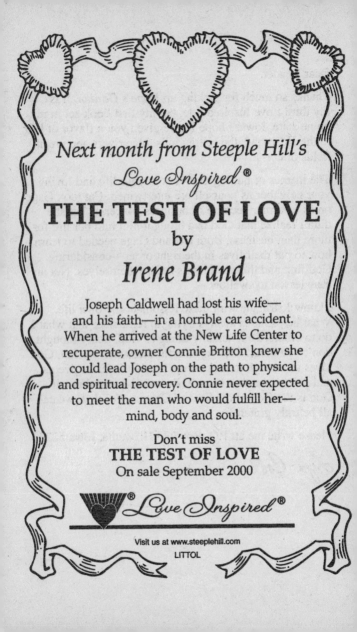